"Stacy, I ~~know the real reason you came~~ **to Kauai," Keith said.**

"You came here to be with me. I know that now." He began humming softly to her. Stacy tried not to listen, tried not to believe there really was magic in the ancient song . . . and in Keith's eyes.

"Stacy, you're so beautiful here. You're like the first woman, and I'm the first man. Here we are together, innocent, in paradise."

"Innocent?" she breathed.

"Innocent of bad intentions, of cruelty, and deception. You know what I am, Stacy, and I know what you are. There will be no guilt in our loving each other."

"You think you know me but you don't—" she began, but he picked her up in his arms, and carried her to a bed of flower petals, their fragrance heady and sweet all at once.

"So beautiful," he murmured, and then he kissed her.

At first she fought the rising flames that threatened to overwhelm her, but then her own need made her respond to his fierce caresses. It was as if Keith had pulled her into a surging ocean of feeling, and an undertow of unexpected power was drawing her out, out, sweeping all she knew completely away. . . .

WHAT ARE *LOVESWEPT* ROMANCES?

They are stories of true romance and touching emotion. We
believe those two very important ingredients are constants
in our highly sensual and very believable stories in the
LOVESWEPT line. Our goal is to give you, the reader,
stories of consistently high quality that may sometimes make
you laugh, sometimes make you cry, but are always fresh
and creative and contain many delightful surprises within
their pages.

Most romance fans read an enormous number of books.
Those they truly love, they keep. Others may be traded with
friends and soon forgotten. We hope that each *LOVESWEPT*
romance will be a treasure—a "keeper." We will always try
to publish

LOVE STORIES YOU'LL NEVER FORGET
BY AUTHORS YOU'LL ALWAYS REMEMBER

The Editors

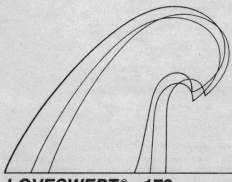

LOVESWEPT® • 173

Nancy Holder
Emerald Fire

BANTAM BOOKS
TORONTO • NEW YORK • LONDON • SYDNEY • AUCKLAND

EMERALD FIRE
A Bantam Book / December 1986

*If you would be interested in receiving protective vinyl
covers for your Loveswept books, please write to this address
for information:*

> *Loveswept*
> *Bantam Books*
> *P.O. Box 985*
> *Hicksville, NY 11802*

ISBN 0-553-21780-1

Published simultaneously in the United States and Canada

PRINTED IN THE UNITED STATES OF AMERICA

O   0 9 8 7 6 5 4 3 2 1

To the entire Loveswept staff,
especially Carolyn Nichols,
with much gratitude, affection, and aloha.
Ha'ina 'ia mai ana ka puana . . .

One

"Anastasia, you don't listen to me! You are missing most beautiful sunset in entire Western world!"

Stacy Livingston roused herself from her thoughts and smiled vaguely at the large-boned woman who was striding beside her on the cliff of sharp, lava rocks. "I'm sorry, Olga. What did you say?"

Olga Kandinskaya frowned. Once Leningrad's top amateur shot-putter, she was now Stacy's best friend and treasured assistant. She was far more massive in build than Stacy, and at five feet eight she was four inches taller. And when Olga looked at Stacy as she did now, she usually made Stacy feel much, much smaller. Like a naughty child, in fact. But at the moment Stacy was too preoccupied to pay much attention to Olga at all.

"Look, Anastasia," Olga commanded. "Such a sight!" She opened her arms toward the horizon and flung back her head in a gesture of pure rapture. "Only in America!" She wagged a finger at Stacy. "And only you with such worry, worry, worry, are missing it like nose on face!"

Stacy sighed, digging her hands into the pockets of her khaki walking shorts. Her curly black hair tumbled over her shoulders as she idly began to look toward the sky.

"Olga, I don't have the heart for rubbernecking. If Keith Mactavish doesn't allow us to look in the caves for—"

She halted abruptly as she took in the scene before her. Her vivid green eyes widened. Below her perch on the lava cliffs, the Hawaiian sun was sinking like a glorious ball of volcanic fire into a bay of tranquil azure water.

"Oh, it *is* beautiful. Olga, it's . . . stupendous."

"What I do tell you?" Olga said smugly, then fell silent as the two of them gazed at the great, gaudy panorama of blazing hues. The shimmering crimson globe was surrounded by halos of dark orange and scarlet, dipping from the cloudless sky into the turquoise sea that lapped the snow-white sands below them. Graceful arches of palm trees enfolded the scene like a rustic picture frame. As Stacy inhaled in wonderment, she smelled the scent of thousands of flowers—ginger, plumeria, jasmine, gardenia—and saw bushes of red flowers that looked like the bottlebrush plants near her apartment back home.

"Is old Soviet saying, taking time to smell flowers," Olga said.

As Stacy wanly chuckled at Olga's unconscious chauvinism, she gathered her hair in her hands and flipped it off her neck to cool herself. It shone in the rainbow sunlight like ropes of jet beads, radiant with blue highlights. Below the wispy fringe of bangs, her forehead was beaded with perspiration. Even in shorts, sandals, and a short-sleeved flowered cotton shirt, Stacy was too warm. Despite the fact that twilight was settling over the mountains and palm trees, the air remained as balmy and moist as it had been two hours ago when they had landed at Lihue, the airport for the island of Kauai.

It was hard to believe she and Olga had left snowy Michigan only eleven hours before. It seemed like days. And now they were only minutes away from their goal—and either the fulfillment of all of Stacy's dreams or the dashing of them.

"I'm too nervous to breathe, Olga, much less smell anything," Stacy murmured, and began walking again. The rickety taxi had taken them as far as it could, but for the last half-mile to their destination they had to go on foot.

"Well, *I* am now smelling cooking," Olga announced a few minutes later. "We must be close to target."

Stacy nodded, and swallowed. Her stomach tightened into a knot as she contemplated the task that lay ahead. "Oh, Olga, what if he won't let us use the caves? My life will be ruined!"

"Not to make mushpot out of molehill," Olga said. "Besides, you are most beautiful ichthyologist in Western world. He will not be able to resist such look of pleading. He will say yes." She smiled. "Believe what I predict. My grandmother was gypsy in Lithuania."

In spite of herself, Stacy laughed. "Olgavitch, you crack me up with your predictions. Do you remember when you held that seance on Halloween? You said I'd be married by this Valentine's Day!"

Olga shrugged. "Is only February second. Twelve more days until Valentine's."

"And I don't even have a boyfriend."

"Don't I know. Break my heart." She sighed and looked at Stacy sadly. "You are twenty-seven years old. Should be married by now, with such small babies."

"You're two years older than me and *you* aren't married."

Olga folded her beefy arms over her chest. "I don't marry until you are safe."

"Safe?"

"*Da.* With wedding ring and honeymoon. Then I grab sexy movie star and become rich capitalist wife!"

"Good grief!" Stacy dissolved into a gale of laughter. "It's hard to believe you've lived in this country for three—" She stopped abruptly as the two of them stepped out of a stand of palms and a tiny ramshackle hut came into view.

"It's nothing but a pile of old boards!" Stacy cried.

"This is world-famous Baggies?" Olga asked incredulously.

"Maybe it looks better closer up," Stacy said as they gingerly walked toward the building.

But Baggies, one of the prime tourist spots on the island of Kauai, actually looked worse as they made their way through the lush undergrowth to a path of cracked stepping stones. The small wooden building was badly in need of fresh paint—it had been white once, Stacy noted—and the sandblasted "Baggies" sign on top of the cockeyed roof was so weathered, it was difficult to read. Boards had been hammered at odd angles, so that the walls looked like crazy quilts of timbers and scraps, the heads of rusty nails nubbing the rough surfaces like knots of thread.

But there was music inside, a loud, raucous rock beat, and a chorus of deep male voices singing "Happy Birthday." And there were laughter and people calling back and forth to one another, and now and then a shrill feminine giggle that pierced through the chaos of the other noises. Despite its wretched appearance, Baggies was, as the guidebooks insisted, "where it's at"—particularly for women tourists, who loved to ogle the sexy waiters it was famous for. The men were all former Waikiki lifeguards, as was their employer, and they made hearts flutter as they smiled and served mai tais, Blue Hawaiians, and, according to *Hawaii on a Shoestring*, truly excellent food.

And if the employees made hearts flutter, their boss made hearts stop, Stacy thought gloomily. He was the one she had to ask the most important question in her life.

She hesitated before opening the front door. "This isn't what I thought graduate school was going to be like at all," she muttered.

Olga patted her on the back. "Only in America," she said, chuckling. "You watch, he will say yes."

Tilting her head, she slid a sly glance at Stacy. "And who knows? Maybe in twelve days you marry him!"

"Right," Stacy said dryly, and pushed open the door.

"Next birthday girl! Come on, don't be shy!"

Keith Mactavish glanced up from the hot stove to watch his burly cousin, Kapono Mo'okini, hoist a giggling woman tourist onto the makeshift stage in the dining room. She was struggling playfully, batting at Kapono's large arms, but it was obvious she didn't mind being the center of attention.

"Come on, pretty *wahine*! You know the house rules!" Kapono insisted. "You gotta dance a birthday hula!" He gestured, and four of the waiters grouped around the stage, one holding a ukelele.

"One, two, three!" Kapono said, and the men began to sing "Happy Birthday."

"Swing those hips!" Kapono directed the woman. "Do the hula, birthday girl!"

"Do it, Marcie!" someone yelled from a table.

"No, no!" the woman cried, laughing and shaking her head. She was pretty, Keith thought, in a conventional, tourist-girl sort of way, with a deep tan and masses of fluffy blond hair. Friendly, too, as he recalled. Like many of the other women present, she had trotted into the kitchen to flirt with him for a little while before "making the scene" in the dining room. That was one of the side benefits, Keith supposed, of his reputation as a busy bachelor.

Turning back to his task, he appraised the fish he was frying, squeezed some lemon juice on it, and flipped it. Done to perfection. He kissed his fingertips like a Frenchman and checked the fillet of *mahimahi* next to it.

Meanwhile, Kapono jumped up onstage with the woman and began to move his hips, urging her to join in. Throwing back her hair, she imitated his undulations, throwing in her own little shoulder jerks. Keith chuckled and put two wedges of pineapple on the two plates beside the stove.

"Very good!" Kapono cried. "Eric, give this brave lady her birthday mai tai! Next birthday girl!"

Keith bent down to check the latest batch of Hawaiian bread in the oven. Rising nicely.

"It's not my birthday!" he heard a woman insist. "Let me down!"

"You were standing in the birthday line," Kapono said. "So you have to dance!"

"It's not my birthday!"

Keith glanced up to see what was going on, but his view was blocked by a group of diners who had stood up to watch the fun. The ukelele twanged the "Happy Birthday" melody as the waiters raised their voices in a ragtag chorus.

"Come on, pretty *wahine*!" Kapono called. "Dance!"

"Please, I'm here to see Keith Mactavish!"

"Aren't we all!" cried a woman in the audience, and when she saw Keith, who had left the kitchen to check out the proceedings, she burst into giggles.

"Hu-la, hu-la!" chanted some of the men.

Keith eased his way through the clump of onlookers. "What's going on?" he asked the tall woman on his left, startled by her size. She was as burly as Kapono.

"Is big mistake, which I am soon fixing." The woman spoke with a thick foreign accent. "They do not make fun of most important ichthyologist in entire Western world!"

He nodded as if he understood, then turned to look at the stage.

And did a classic double-take at what he saw.

The woman standing next to Kapono, pleading helplessly to be spared the ordeal of the birthday hula, was stunningly, gorgeously beautiful. She had hair as black as any Hawaiian *wahine's*, and eyes as green as an Irish lass's. She was pale as snow except for twin spots of flaming red on her cheeks. A *mali-hini*, a newcomer, he surmised, and a very embarrassed one, at that.

But so beautiful!

"Kapono," he said loudly, straining to be heard over the ruckus, "there's been a mistake. Let her down."

But Kapono couldn't hear him. No one could, as they hooted for the poor lady to dance. Keith filled his lungs to bellow his demand that they stop teasing her, then smiled to himself and walked back toward the kitchen. There was a better way to get everyone's attention.

From her place on stage, Stacy watched the blond man disappear back into the crowd. She had hoped he was going to rescue her. *She* had heard him tell the maniac beside her to let her go, even if no one else had. But now he had deserted her.

Too bad he wasn't the rescuing type, she thought. He was certainly handsome enough to be a knight in shining armor. She could tell that even in the muted light of the restaurant. He was tall and built like an athlete, and as bronze as the man on stage. She wondered what his face looked like—it had been too dark to make out his features—but he had the most intriguing silver-and-gold hair, sun streaks on top of moonbeams . . .

Suddenly the clanging of a ship's bell pierced the cacophony. Everyone stopped and turned in its direction.

The blond man appeared in the kitchen doorway. "We're out of food!"

"Hurray!" the cry rose up.

"Free beer!" the man went on. "And we'll have a *hukilau*!"

"Hurray!" At once everyone rushed to the bar.

The man on stage turned to Stacy. "Well, *malihini*, you've been saved by the bell," he said wryly. "My cousin must have taken pity on you. He never can resist a pretty lady." He leaped off the stage and raised his arms to help her down.

She hesitated, then let him. "Thank you," she

said grudgingly as her feet touched the wooden floor. Then, before he could rush off to join the others, she tapped his shoulder and said, "Could you point out Keith Mactavish to me? I need to speak to him."

The man threw back his head and guffawed. "He just saved you from doing the hula," he said. Winking, he pointed toward the kitchen. " 'Scuse me, now. I have to get things ready for the *hukilau*."

The kitchen was in the opposite direction from the bar. Stacy had to struggle upstream through the throngs toward it, and she ran into Olga on the way.

"Is most crazy place!" Olga said wonderingly. "You are sure this is world-famous Baggies?"

"Apparently so." Stacy gestured toward the kitchen. "And that man in there is world-famous Keith Mactavish."

Olga raised her brows. "Oh, for real? Anastasia, he is most handsome!"

"Well, we knew that from reading the guidebook," Stacy said quickly, ignoring the flash of heat that spread over her face. "It also said he was quite the ladies' man, if you remember."

"So? You are preferring he does not like ladies? More lucky for us, so he will say yes to caves."

Stacy rolled her eyes. "Olga, I'm an academic. I don't resort to feminine wiles to get what I want."

"Humph. Sometimes I think you forget you have heart."

"Don't be silly." She smoothed her hair as she glanced toward the kitchen. Keith Mactavish had his back to her—and such a back. He had amazingly broad shoulders, which were emphasized by a blue-and-fuchsia Hawaiian-print shirt. Baggy white shorts clung to narrow hips above long, muscular legs. He wore rubber thongs that had seen much better years.

"I am not silly," Olga said. "I am correct. And—"

"Not now, Olga," Stacy murmured. Her heart was beating as rapidly as it had when she'd opened the restaurant door. It was only nerves, she told herself. Only the prospect of having to speak to him about the caves.

He bent over to put something under the sink.

"Oh." The word became a sigh as Stacy watched the shorts mold his bottom. His buttocks were two small fists of muscle. He obviously didn't spend all day sitting down, as she did.

"Do not be nervous, Anastasia. I am sure he is nice gentleman who will let you on property. Go and ask."

"Okay, okay," Stacy said under her breath, blowing her bangs away from her forehead. "Here goes."

She marched to the doorway and froze. Keith had turned around and was staring at her. Simply staring, without hiding it. When their gazes locked, he smiled slowly, and she thought she would melt into a puddle on the floor. He had the most devastating looks in the entire Western world. His bronzed face was craggy, with angled cheeks and a square hunk of jaw. But it was his eyes that drew her, eyes of the most startling blue she'd ever seen; eyes that caught and held her . . .

"Uh," she blurted. "Uh."

He walked toward her. Her heart skipped a beat. She tried to speak, but no sounds would come out.

He peered at her. "Are you choking?" he asked.

"Ah . . ."

"Do you need the Heimlich maneuver?"

Gathering her wits, she shook her head.

"Sorry about the mix-up out there," he went on easily, nodding toward the stage in the dining room. "We have a birthday custom that's pretty well established, and . . . Are you sure you're not choking? Your face is turning red."

Stacy realized that she was holding her breath. Dizzily she exhaled and took a staggering step backward.

"Are you sick?" he asked in a voice filled with deep concern.

"Kika! I'm going to load up the gear!" called the burly man who'd held her prisoner on stage.

"Okay, Kapono. I'll be there in a minute." He spoke without taking his gaze off Stacy.

"Come here," he said, taking her hand. "Sit down and put your head between your legs."

She stared down at his cinnamon-colored fingers wrapped around her pale hand. "No, I'm fine," she managed to say, but her voice was quavery and faint. She cleared her throat. "Really."

"Let me get you some guava juice."

He herded her into the kitchen and made her sit on a tall stool while he fetched a pitcher out of a wheezing refrigerator. Quickly he poured her a glass of something that looked like pale punch and handed it to her.

"Cheers," he said pleasantly, leaning against a steel sink while he watched her.

She lowered her eyes as she sipped the juice. "It's good," she told him, drinking more.

"We're almost ready, bruddah!" announced the man Keith had called Kapono. He leaned into the kitchen and waved his hand. "Better get a move on."

"Go ahead. I'll take the Jeep," Keith said.

Kapono glanced at him, then at Stacy, and grinned. "Okay. We'll meet down there. Even if we don't really need to go."

Keith smiled back, a little sheepishly. "Well, we're *almost* out of food. And I had to save this poor woman from your clutches."

"Said Bruddah Spider to Bruddah Fly," Kapono drawled, leaving the kitchen.

Stacy saw that the restaurant was emptying out. Men in aloha shirts and women in bright sundresses and short-shorts were filing out of the front door, laughing and cheering.

She took another sip of guava juice. Keith smiled at her.

"Feeling better?" he asked.

"Yes." No. She was so nervous and so . . . something else . . . that she wanted to vanish into thin air. Had he engineered this mass exodus solely for her benefit?

"You and your friend can ride to the *hukilau* with

me." He took the empty glass from her and rinsed it out.

"The . . . what?"

"We're going fishing," he said, taking her hand again. His skin was warm and smooth, and he smelled of coconuts. Stacy forced herself to inhale, exhale, inhale . . .

. . . and exhale.

"We have a tradition here at Baggies," he went on. "When we run out of food, everybody goes fishing, Hawaiian-style. Is this your first time?"

She stared at him. "I beg your pardon?"

He started to say something, but stopped as the strangest expression blanketed his features. He looked bemused, then thoughtful, and he scratched his head with his free hand. "What was I saying?"

"You asked me if this was my first time."

"Oh. Yes. On Kauai."

She nodded. "I came because I . . ." She faltered. Oh, what if he said no? He was too handsome, er, nice, to say no!

"Anastasia, what is happening?" Olga asked from the doorway. "Is bomb scare?" She looked worried.

Keith laughed. "No, no. We're all going fishing. Come on. My Jeep's in the back."

Olga looked at Stacy, who shrugged as if to say, "I guess we'd better go." She clambered off the stool, then followed Keith to the back door, which he ceremoniously held open for the two women to pass through.

"You have asked?" Olga whispered.

Stacy shook her head. "There wasn't time."

"What, no time? Plenty of time!" She grinned. "Time enough for holding of hands."

Stacy sputtered. "Well, you know he's supposed to be a fast worker."

"In Soviet Union, he gets medal," Olga said scoffingly. "Here, he gets big question from you, correct?"

"I'll do it, I'll do it," Stacy murmured, aware that Keith was hanging back so they could conduct their furtive conversation.

"Longer you wait, harder it gets," Olga said. "Same as getting married. She glanced over her shoulder. "Maybe we are killing two birds with one stone with visit to Kauai. I like this cute boy. He has good smile."

Stacy shook her head. "Olga, you're an incurable romantic."

"Anastasia, love is not disease. Someday you must learn this."

"Okay, Olga, I will."

"Longer you wait . . ."

"I know, Olga."

Stacy looked up and stopped stock-still. "Olga, look," she said. Her eyes widened, and she turned to Keith in almost childlike astonishment. "This is . . . words are inadequate."

Dozens of plumeria trees bloomed in yellow and white billows of heavenly scented flowers. There was an orchard of them that stretched as far as Stacy could see. Their velvet petals were strewn like a carpet beneath their branches. Tiny birds darted among the trees, knocking more blossoms to the earth in the still, blue twilight. As the powdery sunlight filtered down on the petals, they seemed to glow as they joined others in small drifts like flurries of magic snow.

Keith put his hand on her shoulder, a move not missed by Olga, who smiled happily.

"I'm glad you like it," he said. He pointed to a small thatched hut nestled among the smooth olive limbs of an immense banyan tree that towered in the distance. "See that little hut? That's my house."

Stacy laughed delightedly. "You live in a tree house?"

"Most of the time."

This obviously disturbed Olga. "Is that not too primitive? What of good light for reading many books?" Which was, she knew, what Stacy spent most of her time doing.

"I use kerosene lanterns," he explained.

"And place to plug in computer terminal?"

Stacy flushed, praying he didn't understand why Olga was asking all these questions. To her, it was obvious Olga was trying to size up his house as a potential home for Stacy.

"Don't they come with batteries now?" Keith asked.

Olga considered. "And for taking of showers, what do you do?"

Chuckling, he gestured toward the ocean. "I have the most beautiful bathtub in the world. Besides," he added, seeing her frown, "there's a shower in the restaurant bathroom. So, do I pass inspection?"

Stacy closed her eyes. He *did* know what Olga was doing!

"For now," Olga answered blithely. "We shall see."

"Okay," Keith said, and took Stacy's hand again. He flashed his white teeth at her as he smiled. "As you say, we'll see."

Half an hour later, Stacy and Olga were stationed along the edge of a gigantic net that Keith, Kapono, and the sexy waiters of Baggies had thrown into the sea. Now everyone was pulling the net back in, harvesting a catch of fish. Flickering torches gleamed golden against the black velvet sky and water and danced on laughing faces and straining arms.

Keith had excused himself from Stacy's side to confer with Kapono, who was his cousin, Stacy had learned. She watched the other women preen and flirt with him as he moved along the line. The edges of the net visibly rippled when he walked by, but he didn't seem to notice. When he saw Stacy eyeing him, he waved. Blushing, she looked away.

She took a sip of beer. The work was making her thirsty, and though she didn't much care for beer, she and Olga were both working on their second cans.

They were also both drenched. They were up to their knees in the warm Pacific Ocean, and the waves splashed them. So did the darting fish, seeking to escape, as they leaped and arced in the slowly shrinking confines of the net.

"I am exhausting," Olga said. "Why you did not ask him back at restaurant?"

Stacy sipped some more beer, knowing it wasn't the tepid water or the work or the beer that were making her skin prickle with heat. "I . . . just couldn't."

Out of the corner of her eye she saw a woman stop and gesture toward the beer Keith held in his hand. She was wearing a string bikini that would've caused a riot—and possibly an arrest—back in Michigan. He let her have a sip, but stepped back easily out of her reach when she tried to kiss him. He mockingly wagged an admonishing finger at her and walked on.

Again he waved at Stacy. Again she blushed and looked away.

But then he took off his shirt. Her body quickened at the sight of all that flesh, perfectly tanned, each muscle delineated as if by the hand of an artist. His chest was covered by a mat of blond hair, which whirlpooled around his navel and plummeted into his shorts. Fascinated, Stacy traced its path, tightening her grip on the net when her gaze rested on the fullness between his muscular thighs.

"What's wrong with me?" she muttered to herself. "I'm acting like a sex maniac!"

"Don't pull so hard!" Olga cried. "You almost knock me over, Anastasia!"

"Sorry. Sometimes I don't know my own strength, Olga," she said between her teeth. But at that moment, she felt positively weak.

"He is good-looking, *da*?" Olga asked archly. "I saw why females swarm around him like flies on apple pie."

A tiny, ladylike burp escaped Stacy's lips. "Really? I hadn't noticed."

"Hah! Anastasia, I *see* you staring at his manly body!"

"I am not!"

Oh, no! she thought. He was coming back!

"Now, ask this time," Olga murmured. "Anastasia, we have come all this way. I am so much jet-logged."

"Olga, *you* ask him."

"*Nyet*. You are chief. I am Indian."

"You look tired," Keith said to Stacy.

"I'm okay."

"We are today from Michigan, United States," Olga informed him.

His heavy blond brows knit together and his full lips stretched into a frown.

"Why on earth didn't you say something? You should be resting!" He pried Stacy's fingers off the net. "You stop, too, Olga."

"I am enjoying," Olga said resolutely. "Please, you take Stacy to sit down while I am doing this." She threw Stacy a fierce look. "She has something to discuss with you, correct, Anastasia?"

Keith looked at Stacy. "You do?"

"Something most important to future of ichthyology," Olga continued, ignoring Stacy who was mouthing a request to cease and desist.

"To the future of what?" Keith asked, cocking his head.

"She will explain." Olga yanked on the net.

"Will she?" Keith's question was directed at Stacy herself.

Swallowing, she nodded. "May we . . . have some privacy?"

For an instant a pleased, predatory expression lit up his face, but it disappeared as quickly as it had appeared.

"Of course." He tucked her arm through his and walked away from the net.

"We'll grab a couple beers," he said, "and then we'll talk."

Stacy's heart pounded in her throat. Her sodden clothes clung to her body, revealing her figure to his darting, appreciative glances almost as much as his absence of clothes revealed his physique to hers.

Keith sauntered over to a trash can filled with beer and ice and grabbed two cans. Together they walked near the fire pit that had been dug to grill the fish. The flames crackled in the silence between them, accompanied by the laughter and singing farther down the beach.

Keith eased Stacy down beneath a lacy palm tree and sat beside her.

"Now, what do you want to talk to me about?" he asked, popping open the cans and handing one to her.

She took a deep breath. This was it, her moment of truth.

"Well, I'm an ichthyologist," she began. "That means I study—"

"Oh, an *ichthyologist*," Keith interrupted. "I didn't understand what Olga was saying. You study fish."

She nodded. "Yes. I'm working on my doctoral thesis at the University of Michigan."

After months of researching old whaling logs and sailors' diaries, Stacy had decided that the Pele's Fire, a beautiful golden fish believed to be mythical, was real. She had based her entire thesis, as well as her academic future, on that assumption. And through her meticulous research, she had traced its spawning ground to two caves called Emerald Eyes, located on Golden Bay, Kauai—and owned by a local family named Mo'okini, of which Mr. Keith Mactavish was a member.

If she couldn't find the Pele's Fire, she wouldn't get her doctorate. It was as simple—and terrifying—as that.

Very close to her thigh, Keith planted his beer can in the sand. Stacy sensed his body heat and casually moved her leg.

"And what do you want to ask me?" He laughed. "I've grown up here and I do a lot of fishing, but I only cook them. I don't study them."

"I know. It's . . ." She swallowed hard. She was starting to lose her nerve again. She couldn't get into Emerald Eyes without the permission of the Mo'okini family. According to the locals, Keith was the family representative on matters like this.

He moved close to her. "Breathe out," he said gently.

She was holding her breath again. As she obeyed, she brought her beer can to her mouth and peered over the rim at him. But suddenly Keith's face blurred, then retreated far away. The palm tree overhead bowed as if it were crashing down on her head. Her hands didn't seem to belong to her, and she watched powerlessly as the beer can fell to the sand and flooded into a pool at her feet.

"Stacy? Stacy?" Keith cried, grabbing her shoulders. "Are you fainting?"

"You have to be as nice as you look," she mumbled before she crumpled against his chest.

She thought she heard him say, "I am, I am!" in a worried voice.

Then everything went dark.

Two

Stacy sighed and threw her arm over her face, sheltering her eyes from the bright sunshine.

Sunshine! But it was dark out!

Or should be. Her eyes flew open and she sat bolt upright.

She was under the same palm tree where she'd talked with Keith. There was a straw mat beneath her and a pillow beside her hand. A light sheet fluttered to her waist.

Had she been here all night?

"Olga?" she called.

A figure glided through the ocean waves, darting through the crests like a sleek dolphin. Assuming it was Olga, Stacy waved. She was rewarded with an answering wave from the figure.

And then he swam toward the shore. Keith, not Olga. Stacy stared as he waded out of the water. The white foam gathered around his chest, caressed his flat stomach and narrow hips. Then he was loping toward her, shaking water droplets from his hair like a big, friendly dog.

"Aloha," he said, dropping down beside her. "Feeling better?"

She touched her forehead. "What . . .?"

"You were just all worn out," he said, touching her hair. "There was a doctor in the crowd who checked you over and said the best thing you could do was rest. So I let you sleep."

She smiled sheepishly. Had the doctor noticed the smell of beer on her lips? "You mean I slept through the *hukinuki*?"

He chuckled, combing her tangled curls with his fingers. Her cheeks tingled where he touched them. "Yes, you did. You were completely oblivious. Olga should be around here someplace too. She conked out an hour after you did." He gave her a stern look. "You should have told me you'd just gotten in."

She smiled shyly. "It seems awfully hedonistic to have slept here all night."

He shrugged. "I do it a lot. I like to have the stars overhead. Fresh air to breathe."

"I'm used to a bed and four walls," she confessed, feeling like a city slicker. So what was wrong with that? She *was* a city slicker.

"But thank you," she added hastily. "And thanks for the pillow and all."

For an answer, he picked up her hand and squeezed it. "I'm a nice guy," he said simply. His words sounded oddly familiar, but she couldn't remember why.

"And you should have told me you wanted to explore my family's caves," he went on. "It would have made everything much simpler."

Her lips parted in surprise. She felt dizzy again—with fear that he would say no. But he was smiling, and she began to hope. . . .

"How did you find out?" she asked.

"Olga."

"And?" Her voice rose with nervousness. Surely he could feel her wild pulse in her fingertips!

"I talked to my grandmother last night. She wants to meet you first, but the unofficial answer is yes."

Her eyes widened, but still she didn't give in to her euphoria. "It's . . . unofficial?"

He laughed and patted her hand. "It's yes."

"Oh, thank you! Thank you!" She was so grateful, so overwhelmingly relieved, that she flung herself into his arms and hugged him. "Thank you!" Then she realized what she was doing and began to pull away.

"Sorry," she murmured.

"Hey, wait a minute. *I'm* not," he said in a husky, gentle voice, and kissed her.

Stacy reared back from the shock of his mouth against hers, her eyes gigantic as the sky, her blood roaring like a waterfall through her stiffened limbs. But his lips were soft and warm, tender and tantalizing as the tropical breeze that ruffled her hair. Spanned across her back, his large hands barely held her, and yet she was unable to put more space between their bodies. It seemed the more she struggled to break the kiss, the more gentle he became. Somehow that was harder to resist than an insistent assault would have been.

She was losing herself in the moment, in his almost protective embrace, in the Hawaiian heat of his body brushing hers. His hard chest was a whisper away from the awakening, delicate points of her breasts. The skin on his arms was warm and smooth and sprinkled with blond hair that caressed her as he shifted toward her, his knees prodding her thighs to open slightly.

"Ah." He sighed. "Oh, Stacy, let me kiss you again."

"Stop," she managed to gasp out, but he silenced her protests with a second kiss.

How could a man be so tender? she wondered. How could such a roughly sculpted face yield such a velvet touch as his lips rolled over hers, then trailed across the hollow of her cheek?

How could he mesmerize her like this?

And then his lips parted and she sensed, rather than felt, the moist heat of his tongue. She was so seized with the anticipation of this deeper, more intimate kiss that she frightened herself and finally pulled away.

As she should have done in the first place.

"I mean it, stop," she said in a rush.

He moved his shoulders. "I have, I have," he said.

Embarrassed, she cleared her throat. "I come from the Midwest," she said uneasily. "We aren't . . . ah, we are a little less . . . casual than you people out here."

The corners of his mouth twitched as he folded his arms across his chest. There were white laugh lines at the corners of his eyes that crinkled when he finally grinned at her. "Is that so?" he asked politely.

"Yes. That is so."

He rocked back on his bottom and clasped his arms around his shins. Resting his chin on his knees, he said, "I see."

"I'm only here to . . ." She stopped, taken aback by the way his blue eyes exactly matched the sea behind him. He was like a spirit of the island, a male siren who seemed to have an uncanny power over her . . . over all women, she added sternly, remembering the way other women had flirted with him the night before.

"To?" he prodded. He narrowed his eyes. "Are you breathing?"

"Yes," she answered in a small voice.

He scratched his chin. "You amaze me, Anastasia."

She blinked. *She* amazed *him*? She wanted to ask him what he meant, but before she could, he laughed and reached forward to take her hands. With a sunny smile, he kissed the back of each one, then sprang to his feet and pulled her up beside him.

"Come on. I want to show you something."

They began to walk toward the water. Then Keith broke into a lope and Stacy ran to match the stride of his long legs. He went faster, and so did she, until finally they raced into the surf.

Laughing, they raised their knees high as the white water broke over their shins. Keith guided her farther out until they were waist-deep in the crystal sea. It swirled and eddied around Stacy's lower body, making her aware of the tension building there, of the sweet sensations she hadn't felt for so very long.

"Stop," he whispered, holding a warning hand in front of her. "There's a coral bed here. Look."

Just below them, delicate fingers of white and pink coral reached toward the surface like the graceful hands of hula dancers. Dozens—hundreds—of small, brilliant fish swam among the coral shapes, their multicolored scales flashing as they darted and dipped.

"I don't need to tell you all their names, do I?" he asked.

She shook her head. "There's Frank, and Sue, and Barbara Ann . . ."

He nudged her ribs. "Cute. I knew you were cute." He grew serious. "I want to kiss you again, Stacy."

She scanned the sky as if searching for something, when all she really wanted to do was keep from looking at him.

"Stacy . . ."

"It won't matter, will it?" she asked uneasily. "About the caves, I mean?"

She glanced at him. He looked utterly shocked and a little insulted. "Are you afraid I'll go back on my word if you don't kiss me?" Her silence was reply enough. "Why, Anastasia! We've already established that I'm a nice guy!"

"We have?"

"Sure. Don't you remember?" He touched the tip of her nose, then combed her hair with his fingers. "I doubt if you'll believe me, but I don't usually go around kissing women I've just met." He looked at her oddly. "I don't usually know them well enough."

"*We* hardly know each other!"

He chewed the corner of his lower lip. "I'm not so sure about that." His brows knit together in a puzzled expression. After a beat, he raised his face to the sun. "I love this place," he murmured, changing the subject. "I never want to leave it again. I'll die here."

"Not soon, I hope."

The sun glittered in his eyes as he slid a glance toward her without moving his head. "No. Not soon. We islanders have the longest life span in the country. Because we don't worry about things," he added pointedly.

She supposed he was implying that she did worry about things. Was it that obvious to a mere acquaintance? But she had a lot to worry about. Her future, for example. What if she couldn't find the Pele's Fire after all?

They stood for a moment in the water. "My grandmother wants to meet you as soon as possible," he said. "She's invited you and Olga to dinner tonight."

"That's very kind of her."

"She's glad for the excuse to have a feast. Tutu loves parties. Everybody in my family does." His face clouded. "Well, almost everybody. So you'll come?"

She was startled by his question. "Of course."

"Good." He looked extremely pleased.

Oh, those eyes, those blue, blue eyes. When he looked at her she felt the same thrill as when he had kissed her. Her body tingled and her hands began to tremble. But how could he elicit such a response in her with a mere glance, a mere kiss?

She told herself it was because she was rusty in the man-woman department. For years she had concentrated solely on her graduate-school studies. Not for nothing was she called "Wondergrind" back in Michigan. Her Friday nights had consisted of trips to the library, where she would hunch over the Hawaiiana collection for hours. Her hot dates were with microfilm viewers and typewriters, not sexy, sun-bronzed hunks. In her sterile, sexless environment, she hadn't developed any immunity to the charming maneuvers of a man like Keith Mactavish. She was defenseless against his invasion of her nervous system.

And oh, was her system nervous. She wondered if he could feel her hands trembling.

Olga would be so pleased, she thought. Then frowned slightly. Where *was* Olga?

A seabird wheeled overhead. Startled, Stacy turned to watch its flight. Then she caught sight of Olga, her best, truest friend in all the world, hiding among the palm trees and watching Stacy with Keith. Watching, not rescuing.

She could almost hear her intoning, "Lithuanian grandmother. I predict."

And there were now only eleven more days until St. Valentine's. . . .

"We'd better go back," Stacy murmured.

"If you like."

Together, still holding hands, they walked through the water. The moment they reached the shore, Olga stepped from behind the trees, yawning as if she had just awakened.

"Such fun barbaric time," she said casually, "sleeping like Cossack on beach."

Grinning wryly, Stacy shook her head. "I doubt the Cossacks ever saw a beach."

"Did so. Turkish peninsula. Anastasia, you are too ignorant of Soviet history."

"I'm sorry, Olgavitch. But at least I know a lot about fish."

Olga shrugged as if to say, "So what?" Then she turned her attention to Keith. "So, you are saying yes to caves?"

"I am. But my grandmother has to formally consent." He squeezed Stacy's hand. "My Tutu Ewa is our matriarch. The Mo'okini men are ruled by our women."

"But you are last name Mactavish," Olga said.

His sunny expression faded, and there was a sadness in his eyes that reached out to Stacy. "It is. But I'm more Mo'okini than Mactavish." He roused himself, the clouds behind his eyes disappearing. "At any rate, I'm sure she'll give you her permission.

She just wants to see what kind of woman intends to explore the hidden secret of Emerald Eyes."

His gaze rested on Stacy's face. "*Your* eyes are the color of emeralds. Are you the spirit of our caves?"

A soft dawn rose glowed in her cheeks. She had fantasized much the same thing about him! "Of course not."

"Don't be too sure," he replied cryptically. "You may be, and not know it. Yet."

"Ah," Olga murmured, and Stacy and Keith looked at her expectantly.

She was beaming from ear to ear. "I have nothing to say," she assured them. "I am daydreaming only." She gave Stacy such a pointed look—*maybe you really will marry him, Anastasia*—that Stacy was certain Keith could decipher it.

"If we're going to see your grandmother tonight, I should get back to the motel. I have so much to do."

Keith laughed. "Such a mainlander. Hurry, hurry, all the time. You're going to give yourself gray hair."

"Not Anastasia," Olga cut in. "She is very calm person, very relaxed. Never worry. No gray hair. And good cook," she added brightly.

"Olga, please," Stacy mouthed silently. "Shut upsky." Olga sighed in response.

"So she's a good cook, is she?" Keith drawled. "Better and better."

Olga rubbed her hands together and regarded the two of them. "*Da*, I think. Better and better."

Keith drove Stacy and Olga back to the modest Rainbow Motel and lingered at their door.

"You know, there are more convenient places for you to stay if you're going to explore the caves every day," he said. "We'll have to see what we can do about that."

"We?" Stacy asked.

"My family." He gestured over her shoulder at Olga. "No, too dressy. We're very casual at my grandmother's house."

Olga nodded solemnly and slipped Stacy's lavender silk dress with the handkerchief hem back on the hanger and put it in the closet.

"Shorts okay?" Olga asked.

"Just great. I'll be back about eight o'clock," Keith told Stacy. "That should give you time to take a nap."

She swallowed. "Is your grandmother someone I need to rest up for?"

"Tutu? She's a darling. You'll love her." His features softened. "And she'll love you." He leaned forward and pecked a kiss on her forehead. "Aloha, Stacy. Olga."

"*Do svidániya*," Olga chirruped.

He sauntered down the steps. Through the window Stacy saw him climb into his ratty old Jeep. It put-putted arhythmically as he disappeared down the road.

"Well," Stacy said, shutting the door.

"You did hear? His babushka is loving you! Oh, Anastasia, I think he is crushing on you!"

"Don't be silly."

Olga held her hand above her head and pointed a finger toward the ceiling. "I predict!"

"You look like the Statue of Liberty, Olgavitch."

" 'To be giving me your poor, your tired, your huddling masses yearning for free breathing . . .' I learn for citizenship test."

Olga flounced on the bed. "Ah, Anastasia, you are remembering how you saved me from KGB?"

Stacy sighed wistfully. "Yes, Olga, I remember."

Olga had been on a goodwill tour of midwestern colleges with some other Soviet athletes when she had defected. Stacy, who had heard of her plight, had offered to hide her in her college apartment. For three weeks she had comforted and looked after the terrified woman while the Soviet authorities dickered with the State Department over her fate. Olga still had bouts of paranoia when she feared that the KGB was after her, though the State Department had assured her she was long forgotten. Besides, her star shot-putting days were over, so there would be no gain for them to snatch her and send her back to the Soviet Union.

"You are remembering how alone I was, how afraid?"

"Yes, Olgavitch."

"Well, I am paying you for that! I am not resting till you are married Western woman! And I think we have hot boy here. I think maybe he will be good husband with large male items."

Stacy burst out laughing. "Olga!"

"Please, I have observed his shorts. I am seeing large size of protrusion."

"Stop it!"

Olga shrugged. "Is true. He will produce good children."

Stacy sank to the bed in a gale of laughter and buried her face in her hands.

"Why laughing?"

"What about his capitalistic tendencies?" Stacy asked as soon as she could speak. "Look at his restaurant. It's a dump! And I'm surprised his car even runs."

"You can rehabilitate him."

"Right."

"Why not right? This is West! Anything is possible. Including wedding in eleven days."

Stacy did not sleep. She paced the small room, tried to read one of the textbooks she'd brought with her, slammed it shut, and paced some more. Through all this, Olga snored loudly enough to shake the rafters.

"I swear, I think you're part Hawaiian," Stacy muttered enviously as Olga sawed away. "You're too mellow to be anything else."

The snoring stopped when Stacy went into the bathroom to get ready for the meeting with Tutu.

She heard Olga mutter to herself in Russian, then call, "Anastasia, you are making self so beautiful for tonight?"

"I'm putting on my makeup," she replied, shaking her head at her reflection. She kept remembering the beautiful women at Baggies who had teased and laughed with Keith—how about that blonde who had done the birthday hula?—and wondered what he saw in her . . . if he saw anything. Maybe he was just passing the time with her because she was going to be exploring on his family's property. *Hawaii on a Shoestring* had mentioned his fondness for the opposite sex. There must be good reasons, she supposed, for "Keith Mactavish" to be listed under "night life"!

"Trust Olga to buy the wackiest guidebook she could lay her hands on," Stacy said, sighing at the smudge of mascara on her lower lashes. Making self so beautiful, humph.

"You must hurry, Anastasia," Olga called. "He should soon be—"

She was interrupted by a "shave-and-haircut" knock at the door.

"It is our boy!" Olga said in a fierce whisper. "He is here!"

"Okay." Stacy tried to stay calm. She touched her hand to her black hair, which she had French-braided into a bundled ponytail, and adjusted the sweetheart-shaped bodice of her green cotton sundress. There was no way she would wear shorts to the home of Keith's powerful grandmother.

"I am getting door," Olga whispered, leaping toward it as Stacy came into the room. Olga was still wearing her bathrobe.

"She is ready!" she announced to Keith. Her eyes bulged, and she turned to Stacy. "Look, Anastasia. Like Michael Douglas."

How could white cotton jeans make Keith look even sexier? Stacy wondered. Perhaps it was the way they molded to his lean hips and muscular thighs, glove-tight around his calves and flaring slightly over tanned ankles and snow-white sneakers. And how could his eyes glow even bluer? Maybe his blue-and-white aloha shirt caught the color and held it, even as Keith caught and held her gaze.

"Good evening, Emerald Eyes," he said. "And Czarina Olga."

"Howdy-do," Olga replied brightly, though Stacy remained silent.

There was nothing she could do to break his spell. She tried to look away and couldn't. She could only stare at him across the motel room. Her heart thumped so loudly, she imagined he and Olga could hear it. Certainly the sound of it thundered in her own ears.

"Your grandmother is waiting," she said at last.

"Not really. She knows we'll show up sooner or later. We islanders have a more relaxed sense of time. Did you have a good nap?" he went on.

"Hah, sleeping, that one?" Olga burst out, then covered by saying, "Oh, *da*, she is sleeping all afternoon. As am I." She made a great show of yawning.

"I am regretting, but I am still so much jet-logged. Do you mind if I remain within motel room and snooze yet more?"

Stacy frowned. "Olga. . . ." *Don't abandon me*, she said with her eyes.

Ignoring her, Olga yawned again.

"It's fine," Keith assured her, flashing the woman a grateful look. Stacy caught it and sighed to herself. Maybe it would just be easier to *get* married, for heaven's sakes, and be spared Olga's endless machinations to get her to the altar!

Married? What was she thinking of? She was too busy to get married. And besides, with her life-style, there was little chance of her meeting someone *to* marry.

She steadfastly avoided looking at Keith as her heart pounded, *Oh, right, Stacy, right . . .*

Keith Mactavish? She laughed to herself. He was hardly marriage material!

She jumped when he walked up to her and put his hand on her shoulder, startling her out of her musing.

"I asked you if you wanted to bring your purse," he said.

"Huh? Oh, yes. Where is it?" She looked around blindly, wishing she could compose herself. But his mere presence galvanized her, and combined with her nervousness over meeting his grandmother, she was dissolving into panic.

"Is here," Olga said, handling her a white straw clutch bag.

"You're sure you don't want to come?" Stacy asked hopefully.

"*Nyet.* I'm too far tired." She smiled a sly, Cheshire-cat smile. "Now go away together."

"Yes, ma'am." Keith pressed a kiss on Olga's cheek and ushered Stacy through the door.

He helped her into his Jeep, and soon they were bouncing down the two-lane highway. Above them, the moon was an iridescent pearl in a sea of midnight blue. As Stacy admired it, the jostling of the vehicle made it bob in the sky, casting undersea moonbeams on the tops of the palms and on Keith's forehead and cheeks. His profile was etched against the darkness like a heroic figure's on an ancient coin.

He took his hand off the steering wheel and patted hers. "Don't be so nervous," he said. "You're among friends."

His touch sent prickles up the back of her neck. She took a deep breath and said, "You don't know what this means to me."

He paused before he replied, "Me neither."

"No, I'm serious. I . . . I have research to do for my thesis." She didn't want to tell him about the Pele's Fire. If word got out, every ichthyologist in the world would descend upon Kauai, eager to take credit for the discovery of a new species. She must guard her quest with the utmost secrecy. It was guppy-eat-guppy in the world of ichthyology.

Keith took a right through a thick stand of trees onto a dirt road. They drove in silence for a few minutes before he said, "Look, let's be honest with each other. I really don't care if you're here to look for the treasure. And neither does my grandmother."

Stacy stared at him. "The what?"

He chuckled. "Oh, come off it. You're planning to search for the treasure of Emerald Eyes. It's okay. In fact, we wish you luck."

Her back stiffened, and she drew her shoulder blades together. "I don't know what you're talking about."

His eyes filled with good humor. "You mainlanders are impossible."

"I am not—"

"Here we are," he said, rolling the Jeep to a stop. "*Auwe*, Stacy, you're stiff as cardboard. Here, let me rub your shoulders."

He reached for her. She drew away. "Let me get this straight. You think I lied to you about why I want to explore the caves."

"You never really said why. Neither did Olga."

"But you know it's got something to do with my graduate-school research."

His hands curved around her tight, hunched shoulders. She could smell his tangy after-shave, like flowers and citrus, only more musky and masculine. "No, I don't know that," he said softly, his thumbs drawing circles along the ends of her collarbones.

"And you think I'm some kind of treasure hunter?"

With expert movements, he found the knots in her muscles and bore down on them. "Aren't we all?" he asked in a low voice. "Doesn't everybody search for their own kind of treasure?"

His fingers were doing enchanting things to her body. The tension, despite her confusion, was seeping out of her. She mustered her indignation and said, "Please. This is a serious discussion."

His smile was lazy, untroubled. "There's no such

thing. This is paradise, *malihini*. We don't have stiff backs and aching muscles here. Or serious discussions."

He cupped her upper arms and began to massage them in steady, slow circles, then found the sinews and traced their outlines with the tips of his thumbs and forefingers. Stacy wanted to tell him to stop, but she couldn't. Instead she cast her gaze down to her lap, watching her fists slowly unfold like blossoms as he eased the resistance out of her.

"If I kissed you now, would you pull away?" he whispered.

"Don't . . ." she said hoarsely.

But he did, and it was wonderful, more thrilling and exciting than the first kiss, if that were possible. Keith lingered at her lips as if he had all eternity to savor them, moving with such deliberation that time slowed, then melted, then ceased to exist. His freshly shaven face was smooth against her cheek, her temple, her nose as he caressed her with the side of his jaw, exhaling as he did so in a languorous sigh of contentment and pleasure. Untroubled, unhurried, he rubbed his warm mouth over hers, parting his lips slightly.

"No," she whispered, catching her breath when his hands moved from her shoulders to her back, pulling her near. He held her in a viselike grip, so unlike his earlier gentleness. For an instant his new strength frightened her, but the fear blazed into a thrill of excitement as he crushed her against his chest. *At last, at last!* her body sang out, and she realized that from the first moment she had seen him, she had longed to feel his flesh against hers. Longed deep inside herself, under so many layers of fretting about her research and her future that she hadn't been able to feel it . . .

"No!" She gasped, trying to pull away.

"Yes, Stacy," he breathed. "Yes." His ocean eyes glowed in the moon shadows as he smiled at her. "Don't you feel it? Something special between us? Something new?"

"Is that the line you use on all the mainland women?" she asked, the haughty ring in her voice surprising her. She was shaken to the core. Yes, she did feel something special, but she was loath to admit that to him, to make herself vulnerable. She hadn't come here to meet a man like him; she had come to do serious research. She didn't need this, didn't want this.

Didn't . . .

"Come on," he said. "You know that's not fair." He forced the full effect of his eyes on her. "Don't you feel it?"

"Please don't pressure me," she pleaded. "I'm not . . . I have so much on my mind."

His smile was so kind, so gentle, it was almost unearthly. Had she thought him a spirit? He smiled like an angel.

"Relax." He traced the worry lines on her forehead. " 'No gray hair for Anastasia,' " he said, mimicking Olga's accent. " 'Very pretty. Good cook.' "

In spite of herself, she smiled back. "She's fibbing about the cook part. At home we live off pizza and hamburgers, unless Olga makes borscht."

"But you do admit you're pretty." His fingers trailed from her forehead to the tip of her nose, which he tapped.

"Oh, yes, simply ravishing," she said ironically. "Men fall at my feet day and night."

"This man is falling." All traces of merriment disappeared from his face. "Truly, Stacy. What I feel is new to me, exciting. I—"

"Uncle Kika! Bombs away!" cried a childish voice, and a shower of jasmine petals rained down on the two of them. The pale blossoms landed in their hair and on their clothes like fragrant confetti.

Keith laughed and shook his head as he brushed off his shoulders. "All right, Lani, where are you?"

"Here, here!" the high voice squealed, and a tiny girl with nut brown skin and hair like Stacy's leaped onto Keith's side of the Jeep. With unrestrained laughter she flung herself into his arms.

"Uncle Kika! I hid a bucket in the tree!" She planted a wet kiss on his cheek, then another, and another. She was like a frisky puppy lavishing affection on him. "I'm so glad you're here! Tutu made coconut pie for you!"

"My favorite," he said, returning all her kisses. He looked over the girl's head at Stacy. "My recipe, too. Lani, this is Miss Livingston. Stacy, my naughty little niece, Lani Williams."

"The lady who's going to look for the treasure?" Lani asked excitedly, casting her shining gaze on Stacy. "Are you her?"

"I'm here to do scientific research," Stacy replied. "I don't know about any treasure."

"But that's silly. Everybody knows about the treasure, don't they, Uncle Kika?"

"As far as I know. But Miss Livingston comes from a long way away, Lani."

"Farther than Disneyland?"

"Much, much farther." He kissed Lani and tickled her under the chin. "Now, go tell Tutu we're here."

"I will. And I'll tell her I saw you kissing!" She slid off his lap.

"Let's keep that part a secret, okay?" Keith asked.

Lani shrugged. "But why? I've seen you kiss pretty ladies before!"

She ran off. With a rueful smile, Keith turned to Stacy and said, "That's my girl. She has a superb sense of discretion. And timing," he added, peeling a petal off Stacy's temple. "Where were we, before we were interrupted?"

"Your grandmother's waiting," she reminded him, hoping to change the conversation.

"And you're a true *malihini*, in a rush to get to business. But I'm not in a rush, Miss Stacy Livingston. There's no sense of time in Eden."

She stared at her hands and saw his instead, covering her fingers, brown on white, so large, they made hers look as small as Lani's.

"There is for me," she finally said. "I have three weeks to find what I'm after."

And eleven days until Valentine's, she heard Olga's voice echo in her brain. *Perhaps you marry this hot boy . . .*

"According to legend, the treasure's been there for over a hundred years," Keith said. "It won't go away."

She balled her hands into fists, drawing away from his touch. "How many times do I have to tell you, that's not what I'm looking for?"

"Oh, I suppose it'll take years to get it through this thick islander skull."

"You're not making any points with me," she said tersely.

He clasped her fists together and kissed her knuckles. "Then I'm an idiot for pursuing this conversation. Let's go see Tutu Ewa, the fire-breathing dragon of Kauai."

They both climbed out of the Jeep. As usual, Keith took her hand and held it as they walked along the dirt path shaded by palms and thick koa trees.

After a few minutes, the road curved around a huge lava boulder on which was painted "Hui Mo'-okini."

Keith chuckled. "That's a little family joke. A *hui* is a sort of business organization like a merchant clan. Tutu's house is our 'headquarters.' "

"But everyone told me to see *you* about getting permission to see the caves."

"That's because they know I can never refuse a pretty woman," he said blithely, then looked as though he regretted his flip reply. But why? Stacy wondered. It was probably true.

"This is it," he announced.

Past the boulder stood a simple house that looked vaguely Oriental to Stacy, with a sloped roof that curved at the ends, and walls of unadorned wood. Coming closer, she saw that it stood slightly above the ground, on stilts.

"It's darling!" she said.

"We call it Menehune House. A *menehune* is our version of an elf."

"Like Lani?"

He beamed at her. "Like you." He tousled her hair. Stacy's scalp tingled and a pleasurable chill slid down her neck.

"Everybody's probably out back on the *lanai*," he went on as they neared the house.

"Everybody?" Stacy echoed.

"Sure. Didn't I tell you? Tutu's called a family meeting. You're going to meet all my relatives."

"No, you didn't tell me." She frowned. "I wish you had."

"Why? So you could be even more nervous?"

"No, so I could—"

Swelling music drowned out her words. A chorus of women's voices, achingly beautiful, rose into the night. Guitars joined in, along with a few male voices, entwining with the crystal sopranos, soaring in a stately song. The voices rose and fell like the tide, then climbed to the heavens and floated above the treetops to the celestial moon, a symphony.

Keith listened for a moment, as transfixed as Stacy, and then he turned to her and sang.

His voice was deep and rich and thrilled her to the bone. He seemed a pagan warrior as he sang the strange, foreign words, a man not of her own world, but of another, more primitive world, closer to the earth and the needs and desires of mortal men and women.

And then the guitars fell away. The men's voices grew louder, the women's more husky, and a compelling rhythm filled this new song, a deep, pounding pulse that found its way into Stacy's blood. Keith's shoulders moved as he sang—no, chanted—as if each syllable were an effort. He sounded as if he were singing a magic spell.

Then, abruptly, he finished. The others did too. All was still, save for the echoing in Stacy's being. He had sung with such fullness, as though he meant every word. A man she hardly knew, singing like that to her . . . She took a deep breath.

No, she mustn't fall under his charming spell, she

told herself. She mustn't forget why she was here, in paradise. . . .

And then a voice from the house surprised them both.

"Well, Kika," said a tiny woman dressed in a crimson muumuu, with a huge white orchid in her hair, "I never thought I'd hear you sing that chant."

She smiled at Stacy. "But perhaps I see why you sang it."

Three

The small woman came down the stairs, meeting Keith halfway as he climbed toward her. They embraced warmly. Then he lowered his head and she kissed the crown of his hair as if she were blessing him. They made a lovely picture—the tall, handsome young man showing respect to the elderly lady, and her shining pride in him as she bestowed her benediction. Stacy was struck by the obvious love between them. Her parents had never shown much affection toward their children, and it startled her when other families hugged and kissed in front of her.

Startled her and made her wistful . . .

"Tutu Ewa, this is Miss Stacy Livingston," Keith said, taking Stacy's hand and leading her up the steps.

"Aloha," Tutu Ewa said. Her chocolate eyes shone as she took in Stacy's appearance. Apparently she liked what she saw. "Welcome to my home. May I call you Stacy?"

"Of course, Mrs. Mo'okini," Stacy replied, gratified that the woman was friendly toward her. Despite Keith's assurances, she still felt that she didn't have

full permission to explore the caves until his grandmother officially gave it to her.

But there was something else in her relief—a definite pleasure that she was liked by Mrs. Mo'okini
simply because the lady was Keith's grandmother.

But why should that matter? What did Keith
Mactavish mean to her? Nothing.

Eleven days, Anastasia.

"Please, you must call me Tutu. Everybody on the
island does."

Stacy smiled shyly. "All right."

"Good. I'm sure we'll get along very well, Stacy."
She reached her hand out to Stacy.

Smiling, Stacy took it. "I'm glad . . . Tutu."

Tutu Ewa slid an approving glance at her grandson, then lifted the skirt of her muumuu and urged
them both up the rest of the steps. "Well, children,
let's join the others. We've prepared a luau in the
backyard and I made coconut pie just for you, Kika."

Keith kissed his grandmother's cheek. "I know.
Lani told us." He laughed. "She rigged a bucket of
pikake to dump on us!"

Tutu Ewa chuckled. "She was picking them all
afternoon. She would have been disappointed if you
hadn't parked your Jeep where you always do. My
grandson is a creature of habit, Stacy. Very predict-
able." She regarded her for a moment before adding,
"Well, usually. Tonight I confess he has surprised
me."

How? Stacy wanted to ask, but she didn't. Instead
she followed Tutu Ewa along the verandah that surrounded the house.

"Later we'll go inside and I'll show you Kika's baby
pictures," Tutu Ewa said mischievously. "He was
such a pretty *keiki*."

"Now, Tutu," Keith warned, "I'm sure Stacy isn't
interested in that." But he looked questioningly at
her as if to ask, *or are you? Have I caught your
eye?*

"Well, time enough for that later," he went on.
"Let's eat. I'm starving."

Tutu Ewa glided in front of them and pushed open a bamboo gate. "Look, everybody," she called, "it's Kika and his friend."

"The treasure hunter!" Lani cried, jumping out of the lap of a lovely, black-haired woman who looked like a younger version of Tutu Ewa.

The back yard was a beautiful Oriental garden with bamboo, a red bridge spanning a creek, and miniature trees grouped in clusters around rock lanterns and stone fences. In the distance, steam rose from a mound, and above it stood Kapono, wearing a chef's apron that read, "I Hate Housework."

A few men and women were standing beside him, dressed in shorts, muumuus, and other casual, colorful clothes, and there were more faces behind the mesh of the enclosed patio. Clumps of children frolicked and shrieked in a rambunctious game of tag.

"My family," Tutu Ewa said proudly.

"*Hui* Mo'okini," Stacy said, and the old lady's face crinkled with delight.

"Exactly. Kika, this *wahine* catches on fast."

By now, other members of the family had begun to rise and saunter over to the three newcomers. The lovely looking woman was the first to reach them, and she smiled at Stacy and said, "Hello. I'm Keith's sister, Maile."

"I'm Stacy."

"Where's Mom?" Keith asked Maile.

"She went to the store to get some more beer. Kapono's drunk almost all of it—with a little help from Brian." She rolled her eyes theatrically. "My husband, Stacy. He's the sunburned one in the polo shirt trying to tell Kapono what to do."

Stacy followed her pointing finger and saw the man Maile indicated, a tall blond who was indeed very sunburned. In his hand he held a beer bottle and was gesturing with it toward the mound.

"He can never remember his forebears were northern Europeans," Maile said, sighing. "He's always lobster red."

"Maybe we should boil him up and eat him," said a stocky man. "I'm Paulo, but you can call me Paul."

"Watch out for this *kane*," Keith said, shaking hands with Paulo. "He's a ladies' man."

"Look who's talking!" Paulo shot back, then looked pained as he glanced at Stacy. "What I mean is—"

"Save it, bruddah," Keith said. "You've done enough damage already. Come on, Stacy. Let me introduce you around."

Stacy met at least a dozen more of Keith's relatives. They had a curious mixture of names and heritages—there were blonds and redheads with names like Doug, Andy, and Mike, and dark-haired men and women named Akamu and Iwone. There was a family of cousins whose last name was Watanabe, and one named Ching.

"We're a real melting pot," Keith said happily, accepting a beer from Kapono and offering one to Stacy. She shook her head—she'd had more than enough beer to last a lifetime—and watched Keith's face light up with delight as he glanced past her shoulder.

"And here's the lady of my life," he said, and for a high, wild second, Stacy thought he was referring to her.

But as she turned and looked, she saw a woman dressed in a blue muumuu, with her dark hair coiled in a gleaming chignon, put down two grocery sacks and wave at Keith.

"Hi, honey," the woman called.

Keith led Stacy over to her. Like a proud father introducing his debutante daughter, he presented Stacy and said, "Mom, this is Stacy Livingston. My mother, Nele Mactavish."

"How do you do?" Mrs. Mactavish said warmly. "You're the girl who wants to explore Emerald Eyes for the treasure."

Stacy shook her head. "Please. No one seems to believe me, but I really don't know anything about—"

Tutu Ewa interrupted her. "Everybody gather around," she ordered. "Nele's back and we're going to have the meeting before we eat."

At once all the men, women, and children began to gather in a semicircle around Tutu Ewa; they lounged on the grass, pulled up rattan chairs, or leaned against bamboo stalks.

Keith winked at Stacy. "As I said, she's our matriarch. We always do what she says—as soon as she says it."

Everyone was assembled quickly. Tutu Ewa nodded her satisfaction and said, "Most of you know why I called a *hui* meeting. This young lady, Stacy Livingston, approached Kika about exploring Emerald Eyes for the treasure."

"No," Stacy began, but Tutu Ewa continued.

"Does anybody mind if she looks for it?"

They looked at one another. Finally Kapono said, "No. Why not?"

Iwone Mo'okini nodded. "I say, power to her if she finds it."

Stacy shook her head in disbelief. "Just a minute. You mean you would let a total stranger dig for a treasure on your property and you don't even care about it?"

The *hui* Mo'okini nodded as one.

"You see, Stacy," Tutu Ewa explained, "we've elevated leisured living to a high art. We don't need much to make us happy."

"We work a little and relax a lot," Kapono added. "What's the point of the rat race?"

"For what, piles of treasure?" Iwone asked.

"For headaches and ulcers, like Keith's father," Nele added, scowling. "My ex-husband thinks he has it so terrific on the mainland, living in the lofty heights of his penthouse in New York City." She gestured around them with the grace of a hula dancer. "Who could ever desert the life we have here for that?"

"Life is too short for endless work and worry," Keith said, summing up his family's philosophy. "And that's what that treasure would bring us. Besides, all those old stories are just tall tales."

Stacy blinked. They really were talking about a treasure! What had she stumbled into?

"What stories?" she asked, and they all looked at one another.

"Surely you've heard them," Tutu Ewa said.

"No. Honestly. I wanted to search the caves for something else."

"Some whaling sailors left a fortune in pearls and jade in Emerald Eyes," said Iwone. "It's one of the legends of Kauai. They say that a whaling captain married one of our great-great-great-grandmothers and took her name as his own. But it all could be just a story. No one knows."

"And no one much cares," Keith added.

Stacy smiled, bemused. "This is hard to take in. I didn't know about the treasure." She felt a flash of hurt when some of the family members traded looks. "No, really, I didn't."

"It doesn't matter anyway," Tutu Ewa said smoothly. "We'll take a vote now." She raised her hand. "All in favor of allowing Stacy Livingston to explore the caves, hands up."

Every person there raised a hand.

"Opposed? Good. The caves are yours to explore as you please, Stacy." Tutu Ewa patted her hand.

Stacy sagged with relief, "Oh, thank you! Thank you all very much. And if I *do* find any treasure— which I'm not looking for, truly—but if I do, I'll be sure to turn it over to you."

"Whatever you think is best," Tutu Ewa said airily. "Now, I'm in the mood for some *kahlua* pig and *poi*!"

So was the rest of the *hui* Mo'okini. Keith helped Kapono unearth a steamed pig from the pit while others set out bowls of *poi*, platters of mangoes, guavas, papayas, and pineapple, along with other island delicacies. The younger set sat on the grass, while the older members of the clan clustered around a picnic table with Tutu Ewa, who led the group in a short prayer before they ate.

Stacy was hungry. She hadn't eaten all day, and

everything tasted wonderful. But she was still so nervous, she found she could manage only a few bites before her stomach tightened. Forlornly eyeing her nearly full plate, she folded her hands in her lap and shifted on the straw mat Keith had spread out for her to protect her dress from grass stains.

Seated beside her, he noticed she wasn't eating. He laid a half-eaten banana on his plate and took her hand. "Can't find anything you like?" he murmured solicitously.

"Oh, no, it's not that," she assured him. "I'm just tired. And excited. I've been so worried . . ."

"Worrying's not allowed here. It's against the law. You must've known you could charm the Mo'okinis into letting you have whatever you wanted."

She smiled weakly. "Olga said the same thing."

"Olga's a smart woman. Also refreshingly direct." He held up his banana. "Here. Take a bite. They're great; made locally."

She hesitated for a moment, then obeyed. As she lowered her head, his fingertips brushed her chin and he smiled at her when she glanced up at him.

"Take another," he urged.

She did. Again he brushed her chin. He had a touch as light as the smoke drifting from the embers in the luau pit. Her stomach gripped and she shook her head, lifting her mouth from the banana.

"Bananas used to be *kapu*—taboo for women." He indicated the shape. "Guess why."

She smiled wanly. "Just as well. I can't eat any more."

"A mango, then. They're not *kapu*."

"No, I—"

He picked up a knife and made two cuts into the large, egg-shaped fruit, then sectioned it away from the pit. He crosshatched the fragrant orange meat, then turned the skin inside out to reveal glistening squares ready to pluck off and devour.

She shook her head. "Really, Keith, I can't."

"You probably didn't eat all day. I didn't notice a

rental car, and that motel doesn't have a coffee shop. On top of no decent rest except a nap this afternoon, you can't skip dinner tonight."

A nap? she repeated silently. Surely he jested. She hadn't been able to stop watching the clock ticking, dragging out the long hours that had contributed to her queasy stomach and wretched nerves. If worrying was against the law on Kauai, she had probably done enough of it to deserve a life sentence, she mused wryly.

Which might not be so bad, came the unbidden thought.

"See? You just went pale," Keith said sternly. "You've got to take better care of yourself."

"You're worrying," she said, and, when he didn't seem to get it, added, "which is illegal here."

He laughed. "Touché. But you've got to admit, *malihini*, you need someone to worry over you."

"No, I don't."

"Or that you'd like someone to worry over you?"

Without thinking, she toyed with her braid. "I have Olga to nursemaid me."

"That's hardly what I meant."

"Mmm." She looked at her full plate so that she wouldn't have to look at him any longer. But she felt the force of his eyes on her, lava-hot and beckoning.

She would not look at him, she would not . . .

But she couldn't help herself. Fighting the compulsion, not able to resist it, she met his gaze once more.

"Stacy," he said, his breath whispering on her neck. "Stacy, what are you doing to me?"

Her lips parted. "I?"

"We have kittens!" Lani cried from the back of the house. "Kika, come see!"

"Lani Pilialoha, you have a great sense of timing," Keith said in a voice meant only for Stacy's ears. He waved at his niece. "In a little while."

"Now!" she pleaded. "They're so *cute!*"

"Don't bother your uncle," Maile instructed. "He's trying to eat."

As if to illustrate his sister's point, Keith picked off a square of mango, lifted it halfway to his mouth, then shook his head and set it down on the plate.

"What's the matter?" Stacy asked.

His eyes gleamed. "Now I can't eat, either. I'm too excited too." His voice was a breathy, bedroom whisper.

She frowned. "I asked you not to pressure me anymore."

A tinge of his mischievous grin appeared, and, as before, his eyes twinkled with merriment. "Where I come from, we don't call this 'pressure.'"

She tilted her head. "What do you call it?"

"Fun. Getting to know each other." He looked as if he were going to say more, but instead scratched the end of his nose musingly and cocked his head.

A warmth like a sunset centered in her stomach, and she felt its colors rise into her cheeks. She had no defenses against him, none, and she felt like an untutored schoolgirl around him—which she was, she supposed. *Gidget Goes Hawaiian. Tammy and the Beach Bum.*

The Saint Valentine's Day Massacre . . .

"Well," she said, "I wish you would stop trying to . . . *pressure* me. It wouldn't be any fun for you, would it, if you won just because I was afraid you would change your mind about the caves?"

He smiled wistfully. "You don't really think I'd play that game, do you? Don't you trust me at all?"

Trust a man who had a guidebook reputation as the island's handsomest—and busiest—bachelor?

He gathered her hands in one of his and rubbed his lips over her knuckles. She swallowed as sparks crackled from her toes to the top of her head.

"Don't you trust me?" he asked engagingly.

"Not as far as I can throw you," she replied, surprised at her own cheekiness.

He chuckled. "How about as far as Olga can throw me?"

"She was a shot-putter."

"Even better."

"Kika! Come see the kittens!" Lani cried. "You can kiss your lady later."

All the Mo'okinis chuckled. Stacy rolled her eyes and raised her shoulders in a defensive gesture.

"Uh oh!" Keith said, reaching toward her shoulders. "You're going to ruin the benefits of my massage."

Stacy rose to her feet. "I'd like to see the kittens, Lani," she said. "Will you show them to me?"

"Sure!" the little girl said.

"You're not playing fair," Keith murmured.

"I don't want to play at all." She started to walk away.

"I wonder." He sprang to his feet and caught up with her.

Kapono said something to Keith in Hawaiian as they sped past him, and Keith shook his head almost angrily.

"What did he say?" Stacy asked. "Was he saying something about me?"

"In a way, but it was really about me," Keith replied cryptically.

"Oh, aren't they *adorable*," Stacy said, cuddling a small gray fur ball against her cheek. It blinked its huge eyes and meowed at her.

Standing in Tutu's back bedroom, the one he had slept in many a night as a boy, Keith regarded these two special females, his niece and his . . . his what? Friend? She certainly wasn't anything more than that. Not yet, anyway.

Oh, but he wanted her to be. . . .

Stacy was standing against the textured wallpaper that Keith's mother had hand-painted with a design of bamboo stalks. She looked like a visiting princess, in her fetching dress and black, black hair, which his fingers itched to unbraid and spread over her creamy shoulders. The careful, loving way she petted and fondled the kitten belied an inner warmth he had known she possessed, but which she still hadn't shared with him.

"It's so precious," Stacy said, sitting on the old double bed covered with a quilt Tutu Ewa had sewn.

"You can have it if you want," Lani said, handing a kitten to Keith. "Tutu wants me to find homes for all but one of them."

"I wish I could." Stacy nuzzled the kitten's front paws with her nose. "But there's no way with the plane and all."

From out of nowhere, Keith felt a strange tugging at his heart. Puzzled, he frowned. Now, what on earth was that sensation? It was almost like sadness. Loss.

Worry.

"At least you can name it," Lani suggested. "It'll be like your kitten even when you're gone."

Gone. Keith stared at Stacy. The tugging had to do with the thought of her leaving.

Oh, but that was stupid! Of course she would leave. She was a mainland woman, like all the others he flirted with and sometimes invited into his tree house.

Wasn't she?

Oh, more beautiful than most, and certainly more driven. But there was nothing special about her.

Was there?

He already knew the answer to that. He'd even told her as much. He frowned harder. What on earth was happening to him?

"Uncle Keith!"

He stirred. Lani and Stacy were pointing at him and shaking with laughter.

"What?" he asked, completely baffled by the emotions churning inside him. Too much beer, he decided. Too much of something, anyway. And not enough common sense.

"What?" he asked again.

"Don't you even notice?" Lani demanded, and both she and Stacy began to giggle again.

"The kitten!" Lani pointed at his leg.

Such a young kitten, of course, was not housebroken. And had just proved it all over the left thigh of Keith's white jeans.

"Oh, for heaven's sake," he said, mortified.

"You didn't notice!" Lani crowed. "We were both yelling at you to put it in the box and you didn't hear us!" Giggling, she tweaked his nose. "And you're turning red. Oh, Uncle Kika!"

"You'd better take them off," said a voice from the doorway. It was his sister, Maile. "We should wash them as soon as possible."

"I'll be fine," he insisted, glancing at Stacy. Like Lani, she had the giggles, but there was also a strange expression on her face. Curiosity, perhaps, or wariness, or was it . . . hope?

"No," Maile said. "Take them off. We must have a spare pair of pants around here somewhere."

"Nobody wears his size," Lani said. "He'll have to wear one of Tutu's muumuus."

"Nonsense. He can just wrap a *lavalava* around himself."

Keith nodded. That would be fine with him, if all these women would stop eyeing him so intently. He felt as if he were in a doctor's office, and everyone but he knew that he'd contracted a disease.

"I'll change in the bathroom," he said gruffly. "Maile, please bring me a *malo* and I'll put it on."

With that, he stalked out of the room and crossed the threshold of the bathroom, but not before he heard Maile say, "Lani, I think your Uncle Kika's met his match."

And Stacy replied, "What are you talking about? The kitten?"

Holding open the door, Keith paused. So did Maile, before she said, "Yes, Miss Livingston. I meant the kitten."

But Keith recognized the lilt in Maile's voice that betrayed her when she fibbed. The kitten was the furthest thing from her mind . . . as it had been from his.

A disease.

"Humph," he said, and went into the bathroom.

He emerged a few minutes later with his lower body wrapped in a brown batiked length of fabric. The look on Stacy's face made him suddenly very grateful to the kitten for having an accident on the jeans. She had given him the once-over while he wore those, but the effect of the *lavalava* was more than he could have hoped for. She was mesmerized.

Auwe, but her eyes were green. Green as a crisp dollar bill, his father would say. Keith sighed. He hadn't seen Gerald Mactavish in almost two years, and he tensed with the remembered strain of their last meeting. Keith had turned down Gerald's offer to become a partner in his real-estate-development company, and Gerald had been stung. "You're just like all those other bums!" he'd railed at his only son. "Lying around on the beach all day, when there's money to be made, opportunities to exploit. How I ever got involved with those people is beyond me, but it kills me to see you going native, Keith. It just kills me."

Well, that was the past. And this was paradise, where fretting was not allowed.

He grinned at Stacy, who was still eyeing his legs, though she pretended to fuss with the kitten.

"So, do you think it'll play in Ohio?" he asked lightly, posing for her.

"I'm from Michigan," she replied. "It's snowing there."

He shivered. "Ick."

"I like a change of seasons."

"We have seasons. Sometimes it rains more than others." He laughed. "Of course, Kauai is one of the wettest spots on earth."

As if on cue, rain pattered on the roof. They both looked up.

"I hope Olga's inside," Stacy said.

"It's warm rain," Keith reminded her. "She won't be the worse for it. Here in Hawaii, we take it in stride—literally. We don't even stop walking to find shelter. So you see, I don't really even need a shower," he went on, referring to yesterday's conversation at the restaurant. Good grief, had he known her for only a matter of hours? It seemed he had always know her. Again something tugged at his heart.

"But seriously, folks, " he added, "if you can stand a tepid downpour, I'd like to suggest that we take a little walk."

Oh, he thought, look how her defenses rose up like the walls of a fortress. He wished he were small and fuzzy and liked Cat Chow.

"You'll like this walk," he promised, hoping he looked earnest. "It will make your day." Boy, did *that* sound leading.

"Oh, really?" she drawled. "And just where do you want to take me?"

Anyplace she would allow, he said to himself, but to Stacy he widened his eyes with mock innocence and replied, "Oh, just to a couple of caves my family owns."

She inhaled so sharply, the little kitten squalled. "You mean to Emerald Eyes?" she asked, stepping toward him. For a moment Keith thought she was going to fling herself into his arms, the way she had that morning when he'd given her permission to explore the caves.

Imagine, only this morning . . . All through the day he'd replayed those wonderful kisses of hers, and dreamed of getting more of them. Thus far, he had not been disappointed.

But this time Stacy held herself in check. Though her body leaned toward his, she pressed the kitten against her chest—lucky animal—like a shield.

She was so wary that it pained him. Before he could stop himself, he placed a hand on her arm and murmured, "Stacy, please. You make me feel like an old lecher. It's impossible not to flirt with you, but every time I do, I feel like I'm committing a crime. Do you mind it so very much?"

Her eyes flickered, and she lowered her gaze to the

kitten. Keith thought he heard a mumbled "no," but he wasn't sure.

"Stacy?" he prodded.

"Let's go see the caves," she said, raising her head. Her cheeks were bright red.

To Stacy, walking through the dense growth behind Tutu Ewa's house was like strolling through a florist shop. Ferns and flowers dripped silver from the recent downpour, liquid moonlight that slipped down vines and pooled in little ponds beneath lush branches.

Keith was barefoot and didn't seem to notice the tangles and brambles that pulled at Stacy's panty hose. She hadn't planned to wear stockings, but after seeing everybody's championship tans at Baggies, she was embarrassed to display her winter-white legs.

His legs were dark and sinewy, like a full-blooded Polynesian's, and he moved with the grace and ease of a jungle cat.

And he was like a cat, she thought, delighted as he put his hand on her waist to guide her out of the way of a spreading palm frond. Playful and easygoing, but a hunter and predator too. Eyes that watched you intently, teeth that flashed to impress and disarm you. He possessed a feline grace, and sometimes when he laughed the sound was almost feral.

What would it be like, to be captured by him?

"Come here, Stacy," he said softly, beckoning her from her thoughts. He was standing a few feet away from her, hidden from the moonlight by the trees that towered above him.

She obeyed, and for a moment she thought he was going to kiss her, and that she was going to let him. Instead he parted the trees and said, "Madam, your gondola awaits."

Beyond the trees, the moon reflected on still, glittering water that stretched to a distant bank. Just below Stacy's feet bobbed a weathered red dinghy.

"We have to row in," Keith explained. "The caves can only be reached by water."

She nodded. "Yes, I know. I've researched these caves extensively."

He narrowed his eyes in mock suspicion. "Then of course you read about the legend of Captain Kale's treasure."

"No." A twinge of distress made her forehead wrinkle. She thought she knew everything about Emerald Eyes. What if she were wrong? What if the Pele's Fire didn't spawn there in three weeks? Her academic career—the only thing she cared about—would be ruined.

"Not even one small mention?" he asked.

"I told you, no!" she snapped. "Why doesn't anybody believe me? Why do you all keep insisting that I'm lying?"

"Easy, easy." He kneaded the back of her neck. "You're tied in knots again. You're a very intense person, you know. Haven't you read all the articles about Type A personalities? You've got to take life easier."

His fingers urged her shoulder muscles to slacken, her spine to unbend. As they relaxed, she became aware of other muscles that were sore and stiff—her upper arms, her lower back, even her thighs. For almost a year she had been under incredible pressure, which was far from over.

"You don't know anything about me," she said defensively, climbing into the boat as he held her hand.

"Bet me. I know you could use a good massage." He gave her a cockeyed grin. "And I just happen to be a great masseur."

"Let's just go, all right?" Her voice sounded shrill, and she was immediately embarrassed. "I'm sorry. You're right. I'm very uptight. I've put all my energy into this thing and I still have a long way to go."

He untied the dinghy and climbed in. She sat facing him, and as he settled in and gripped the oars, she saw a flash of white underwear beneath his *lavalava*. Swallowing, she shifted her weight and crossed her legs at the ankles.

"I must sound like I'm lecturing you," he murmured. "I'm sorry, Stacy. It's just that I see no point in stomping grimly through life. I believe we were put here to enjoy ourselves. To me, unhappiness is about the only sin there is."

"And I'm a firm believer in the Puritan ethic," she said. "Talk about opposites."

"You know what they say." He dipped the oars into the water. The boat glided away from the bank and into gauzy moonbeams.

"What do they say?" she asked.

"That opposites attract."

Stacy looked to her left and studied the placid water. Shapes darted to the surface, casting rings that rippled and grew, then faded.

"Well, they do, you know," Keith said.

She glanced at him. "How would you know? You're attracted to everyone."

"I . . ." He paused, looking frustrated. Probably because he had enough integrity not to deny the truth, she decided.

"There would've been a time when I would have agreed with you," he said finally.

She flushed, because she still believed she was right despite his reply. Knowing that he would treat other women exactly the way he treated her made her feel like one of a herd, and not someone special to him.

But she didn't want to be special to him. She wanted to do her research and hightail it back to Michigan to work on her thesis. If, merciful heaven, she had anything to write about.

"Stacy?"

"I'm sorry. I'm fading," she said, only half-lying. "That plane ride took a lot out of me."

"Maybe we should have done this tomorrow. But I knew you were eager to see the caves."

"Thank you. I do appreciate it."

They moved from light to shadow and back to light. Keith's eyes were two lagoons of blue as he studied her. The only sound was the pleasing dipping of the oars into the water and an occasional creak of wood.

She watched his body flex and contract as he rowed. What would it be like to touch him?

To make love with him?

"Look," Keith said, pointing behind himself. "We're there."

Four

On the right side of the dinghy, two large caves jutted from a fork in the horseshoe-shaped bay. They looked like giant eyes set close together with a nose of lava between them.

"In the daytime, the green water looks like irises," Keith said. "Some people say the surrounding land is the face of a sea goddess. She's standing on the bottom of the world and watching us mere mortals to make sure we respect the creatures of her kingdom."

"I can see what you mean," Stacy said. "It does look like a face." Her heart was pounding. This was it! Emerald Eyes!

"Eerie, isn't it?"

"Beautiful," she breathed. "Absolutely breathtaking."

"Yes," Keith said quietly. "Absolutely."

"I wish we had a flashlight." She raised up on her knees and tried to peer into the blackness.

At her words, a beam of light pierced the shadows. Surprised, she saw that Keith was holding a small silver flashlight. He pointed it at a sack at his feet, which he opened with one hand.

"Lantern," he said, showing it to her. "Rope, shovel, pick, Polaroid camera. Champagne."

"Champagne!" she cried.

He flashed the light on the label. "Moët et Chandon. Only the best to celebrate our mutual good luck." When she looked at him questioningly, he explained, "Your being allowed to explore our land, and my meeting you."

She wondered if he could see her smile. "I haven't tasted champagne since the day I got my bachelor's degree. I'm your proverbial starving student."

"You look great to me. Of course, Tutu wants to fatten you up. Did you know that *her* grandmother weighed almost three hundred pounds? She was considered very beautiful in her day."

Stacy realized as he spoke that Keith and his grandmother had talked about her, and she felt an odd, warm sensation as she imagined their conversation. At school, she tended to think of herself as invisible, a slaving graduate student whose presence merited not the slightest notice. Sometimes she imagined herself a mole, creeping around the musty library stacks, ferreting out information like a little black-haired weasel. But here, the only person who knew her in that way was Olga. To the Mo'okinis, she wasn't even an academic. She was—how exciting—a treasure hunter.

"Well, if it's any consolation, my mother thinks I'm thin too," she said.

Keith rowed the dinghy toward the mouth of one of the caves. "Does she think you study too hard?"

Stacy frowned. "She doesn't really know what to think of me. I've been a 'grind,' you might say, ever since junior-high school."

"I don't follow."

She shifted, growing uncomfortable. She didn't want to talk to him about her past, but there was real concern in his voice, and somehow, words began spilling from her mouth.

"We're very poor, you see. I think my father was frustrated by having so many children. . . . Anyway, he's critical of us all. It wasn't until I started getting good grades that he praised me much. . . ." Her voice trailed off. "This sounds so maudlin. Let's open that champagne."

She reached for the chilled bottle; he let go of the oars and covered her hands with his. "No. Tell me the rest."

She shrugged. "There's not that much more to tell. I saw education as a way to earn his love and to escape poverty. From the time I was twelve, I studied almost all the time. I desperately wanted a scholarship to college, you see. . . ." She forced a laugh. "I'm getting depressed. Let's change the subject."

There was a long pause. Then Keith said, "Here, take the flashlight. We're going to enter the cave to the right. And as soon as we tie up, we'll open the champagne."

Embarrassed, she obeyed. She had said too much, she assumed, and had embarrassed him too. After all, this was paradise, where the happy natives played all day and laughed at fretful outsiders. She didn't suppose Keith's childhood had been unhappy. Except, she recalled, that his parents were divorced. She wondered how that had come about.

Then they were crossing the threshold of the cave. Stacy scanned the darkness with her flashlight, then gaped at what she saw. The water cast green reflections on the walls and the ceiling of the cave. The boat seemed to move in slow motion, adding to the tantalizing illusion that they were underwater, guardians sent by the sea goddess to oversee her domain. Farther on, a small waterfall shimmered on surrounding banks of lush ferns, the steady stream of water creating a distant background sound to the throbbing of Stacy's heart. Rocks were piled atop one another to create the semblance of a long semicircular bench, and to the left of it, a passage disappeared into the wall of the cave itself.

"It's fantastic," she said. "Better than I imagined it. And nobody mentioned the waterfall."

"It's just a little one," Keith said. "Probably caused

by decades of erosion that took place after the accounts you read were written."

"Probably so. I wonder what else has changed." Had those whalers really seen the Pele's Fire? she wondered. Did it still exist? Would it return, as she had predicted?

"You're much more subdued about this than I thought you'd be," Keith said, guiding the dinghy near the benchlike shape. "I was hoping you'd throw yourself into my arms again."

"I was wondering about Olga." She was lying, still intent on keeping her reason for being here a secret. "She'll probably go out to get something to eat. Even though she's been in this country for three years, she still has a little trouble on her own. When she gets flustered, she forgets her English."

"I suppose you'll want to go back soon." He sounded disappointed, and she was sorry for it. But he was wrong. She wanted to stay inside the caves all night, exploring them, seeing firsthand what she'd read about.

"Well, actually . . ." she began, but stopped speaking as Keith stood and put one foot on the jutting boulders. He seemed to be having trouble pulling himself up.

"It's slippery," he said. The boat rocked as he tried to maintain his balance. "But I think with just a little more—whoops!"

Arms flailing, he fell back into the boat, rolled over on the other side, and overturned it.

"Grab the champagne!" he cried as Stacy tumbled into the water.

Thinking he wanted to prevent it from beaning one of them, she obeyed—and realized too late that she should have concentrated her efforts on retrieving the flashlight or the oars.

Hugging the champagne to her chest, she trod water and flailed around, trying to find the side of the capsized boat. "Keith?" she called. Her blood chilled when there was no answer. "Keith!"

A moan issued from the black water. "I hit my head," he said, groaning. "I think I'm bleeding."

"Oh, no!" she shouted. "Where are you, Keith? Can you swim toward me?"

Warm fingers slid around her waist. "Here I am." The fingers crept up her stomach and hit the bottom of the bottle. "You have the champagne."

"A lot of good that will do us," she said, straining not to betray her instant response to his touch. Her breasts were tingling, the nipples contracting to delicate buds, and she half-consciously willed his fingers to fondle them. When he didn't, she carefully let out her breath, and added, "I should've retrieved something more useful. Do you think we can turn the boat over? We should get you to a doctor."

"It's not that big a deal," he said casually. "What I'd really like to do is rest for a while. The dinghy will float, even upside down. Let's just climb up the rocks. There's a ledge under the water someplace. . . . Ah, here it is.".

He put his arm around her waist as he stepped onto the ledge. Pressed hip to hip, he held her tightly, as if making sure she didn't slip back into the water. His body was hard, his hip a square of bone and muscle, contrasting with her feminine curves. His arm stretched along her back and gripped her side, just brushing her breast. She began to tremble, not from the dousing in the warm Pacific water, but from his nearness. She wondered if he could feel it.

"Now you climb up and I'll find the boat line," he said. When she hesitated, he patted her hip and added, "Don't be afraid."

"I'm not," she retorted, mildly insulted. "I think it would be better if you climbed up and I retrieved the line. You might have a concussion. What if you sank underwater and passed out?"

"But I don't . . ." He sighed. "Okay. You have a point. But I want you to be careful. In fact, I'll stay here until you find it. Then we'll climb up together."

She was dubious. "I still think we should go back

as soon as possible. For all we know, you may be seriously injured."

"I'm not."

"But—"

"Please, Stacy. Just find the line."

"Oh, all right."

She sank back into the water and found the hull of the boat, then felt downward until she located the rope attached to it. She emerged triumphantly, holding the line out, then realized that of course he couldn't see it in the blackness.

"I have it," she said.

"Good. I'll tie it to a boulder." He took the rope from her and set to work. "Okay. I think that's secure. Come on. I've found an easier way to climb up."

It took about a minute to scramble up the rocks. On top, they were surprisingly smooth, and it was comfortable to sit down on them with outstretched legs.

"I feel like Robinson Crusoe," Stacy said, then jumped when she heard a noisy pop.

"The champagne's uncorked," Keith announced. "To Stacy. May she find whatever she's looking for."

The tip of the bottle poked her side. She hesitated before accepting it, then said, "And to Keith. Who has a bad sense of balance." She took a sip. "It sure beats instant coffee."

His fingers closed around hers, and he held them there as he lifted the bottle to his own lips. "You're right there, but then, I rarely drink instant coffee."

"I don't have time at home for much else." They were sitting close together, their legs pressed against each other's, and Stacy found she was having trouble breathing. She wanted to move away—didn't she? —but she didn't want him to notice that she was doing it.

"I don't have time to bother with instant," he said. "It's pure Kona dripped or nothing."

"I usually get mine out of a vending machine on the way to class. I'm also a teaching assistant."

"You lead a hectic life," he said. "Your turn for a sip."

She could smell him now, salty and tangy and desirable. When he held the bottle toward her she sensed his warmth, and a pulse point deep inside her began to thrum with excitement.

"We probably shouldn't drink any more. Your injury—"

"It's just a little bump. Here, feel it."

His thumb spanned across her fingers and arched them slightly. She waited for the sensation of touching his wet forehead, but instead her fingertips pressed against his lips, surprisingly dry, wonderfully smooth, and very, very tempting.

"Now, stop this," she murmured unsteadily.

"What's that, love? I didn't hear you."

"I said . . ." She swallowed. "Keith, don't tease, now. You may be hurt."

"Pierced by Cupid's arrow?"

"Must you have such a one-track mind?" Her voice was a wail and a plea, but Keith answered it with a throaty chuckle.

"What's so funny?" she asked. "Why don't you listen to me?"

"You ask too many questions, mainland lady. Perhaps if you sit still, you'll get some answers."

Again he pressed her fingertips against his mouth. He parted his lips slightly and sucked on her forefinger. A sharp quiver vibrated through Stacy, and she inhaled to stifle a gasp of pleasure.

The somnolent waterfall trickled in the throbbing stillness between Stacy and Keith. Could he hear her heart? she wondered. Could he read her confused thoughts and jumbled emotions?

"Stacy, you know I want you, and I believe you want me. I've seen you looking at me, and your eyes never leave my body. You watch me when I walk and bend and move, just as I watch you. We're like two animals circling each other, waiting for the right signals to begin the mating dance. There's nothing wrong with sexual desire, is there? I mean, people do make love in Ohio, don't they?"

"Michigan," she managed to say. Inwardly she was struggling to deny the truth of his words . . . and failing.

"Don't they?"

"That's not the point." She shut her eyes tightly as he sucked on her middle finger, grimacing as she fought the tide of pleasure that threatened to wash over her. Her body burned as if she were sitting too close to a fire . . . which she was. The fire goddess Pele was not the only Hawaiian who commanded the forces of nature. What she felt for Keith was the awakening of an elemental need that surged strong and deep beneath her surface. She had never thought of herself as a sensual being, but as an intellectual, and Keith was forcing her to take another look. To feel another sensation. To hunger for him yet again, as she had since the moment she saw him . . .

"I . . ." *hardly know you*, she had planned to say, but she knew he would answer with something like, "What better way to get to know each other better?"

Perhaps she was old-fashioned, expecting that sex was an expression of deep, abiding love and commitment, of a relationship destined to flower and grow over time to a garden of earthly delight. She had never had, nor ever wanted to have, a one-night stand, or a "quickie," as some of her friends called it. She wasn't interested in sex for sex's sake. To her, making love with someone should be just that: making *love*.

But then, why did she want him so much? A total stranger whose name she barely knew?

In the darkness, Keith sighed. "Have some more champagne," he said, nudging her with the bottle as he released her captive finger.

"Are you trying to get me drunk?"

"A little relaxed, maybe. You could use relaxing, you know."

"So you've told me. Many times."

"I've never felt shoulders as knotted as yours."

Her breath came more easily. He was backing off. If only he'd known that a few more silky words would have mesmerized her into capitulation. But he had given up only seconds too soon.

"It comes from hunching over books, I suppose," she said.

"Well, it's too dark to read here, thank the good Lord. And you didn't bring a book anyway. So lean back, breathe deeply, and enjoy the night. And take another sip."

Stacy hesitated. "I'm not used to drinking so much. After last night . . ."

"That was jet lag, not beer. You're not going to pass up fine French champagne, are you?"

"I really shouldn't."

"That's a *kapu* word here. We never say 'should.' It causes wrinkles and backaches. Now, tell me you don't want any more champagne, and I'll be content."

She wrinkled her nose. It did taste awfully good.

"Maybe just another little sip," she said.

He laughed. "All right."

Outside the cave, Hina, the lady of the moon, trailed her train of stars across the heavens. Pele was silent, and her sister, Laka, goddess of the hula, danced in the midnight sky with the palm trees and the surf.

Beneath the water, night rainbows of fish fluttered and leaped toward the cave, then into it, and dove down deep to sniff, in their fashion, at a sunken lantern, camera, and flashlight.

Then they poked their heads above the surface to nibble on the toes of a man and a woman who had scooted to the edge of the rocks to dangle their legs in the water.

"Oh, they tickle!" Stacy laughed, kicking her feet. She took another swig of champagne.

"They're kissing you," Keith said, accepting the

bottle from her for his turn. "Just like I'd like to be doing."

Though he couldn't see her, she wagged her finger at him. "Uh, uh, uh, Mr. Hukinuki. Keep your *lemus* to yourself."

He guffawed. "Want to try that word again?"

"Your *lemu*," she repeated, covering her mouth to staunch a bubbly burp. "This bottle's almost empty!"

"Sorry I didn't bring another."

"Hah. Yeah, I'll bet."

"*Lima* means hand," he said.

She frowned to herself. She felt so dizzy! And so silly!

"I thought that was what *lemu* meant," she said.

"Nope."

"Well, then, what's a *lemu*?"

He chuckled. "A buttock."

"Oh." Heat flamed her cheeks. "I've had too much to drink."

"I'd say you've had just the right amount." His tone was amused and warm. "I just hope you don't get a headache later on. But Tutu has a home remedy for hangovers that's helped me out on occasion. She's a true *kahuna*, a medicine woman."

The cave rocked. "*Kahuna. Lemu. Lima. Ule.*"

Again he laughed. "I didn't teach you *ule*!"

It seemed such an effort to talk. She wanted desperately to lie her head in his lap and go to sleep. Oh, to have him rub her neck and shoulders! He was right; they were always sore and tight. She had never noticed it before, but now they bothered her constantly. "What's *ule* mean?"

"It refers to something I have that you don't."

"Nerve." She giggled.

"Not exactly. It's located a little lower."

She covered her head with her hands. "Oh. Oh, my goodness, I'm tipsy. Two nights in a row. I'll never live this down."

He patted her knee. "Don't worry. I have a feeling you won't even remember it, you dear baby. I didn't realize your tolerance for alcohol was so low. Didn't Olga teach you how to swig vodka?"

"Olga," she murmured, stirring. "She'll be worried sick!"

"I'm not so sure about that."

"What do you mean?"

"Well, you're a woman and I'm a man, and I think our mutual attraction is pretty evident to anybody who sees the two of us together. I suspect Olga would assume you're spending the night . . . else- where."

"No. I never do. I don't at home," she said without realizing what she was revealing to him.

"Ever?"

"Unless I fall asleep in the library." She laughed again. "See? Some fun date, huh?"

There was silence for a moment. "Come here," Keith said, tousling her hair. He pressed her head against his shoulder and wrapped his arm around her, snuggling her against him. With great care he lifted her feet out of the water and eased himself and her away from the water's edge.

Her entire body prickled with electricity. The hair on her neck stood on end, and her lips and fingers tingled as if they were numb. Gasping, she demanded, "What're you doing? What?"

"Ssh. I think it's time for one Stacy Livingston to get some sleep." He sighed heavily. "Unfortunately."

After a few minutes the wild sensations subsided, and in their place Stacy felt an overwhelming need to sag against him and close her eyes. At last she was wrapped in his warmth, as she had longed to be.

"At last," she muttered.

"What, honey?" he asked, pressing his ear to her lips.

"Fading fast."

"That's okay, Stacy. Go right ahead. I'll take care of you."

"So embarrassed."

"No need. I know you're not a little boozer in real life."

Real life. What was real life? she wondered hazily. Was there really a place called Michigan? Where there were hard wooden seats and musty books, and freezing sleet and instant coffee?

No, there had never been. Real life was sunshine and flowers and laughter. And blue, blue eyes . . .

"Treasure," she whispered.

"Tomorrow we'll start looking. Now, go to sleep."

Drowsily she draped her hand over his shoulder, pure polished stone. He was the kindest, dearest man in the world, to watch over her in her drunken stupor. The kindest, dearest, most handsome . . .

"G'night, Kika," she murmured, floating away.

He sighed again. "Good night, Emerald Eyes."

An hour passed, then two. Stacy would stir, almost come to the surface, and fall back into sleep. And in between those times, she would drive Keith senseless with desire.

Three hours passed. Keith grimaced as Stacy unconsciously played with the hair on his chest. She was smiling dreamily and scraping him with her fingertips, and he was becoming so aroused, he had to bite his lower lip not to cry out.

Well, it was his own fault for pulling this stunt, he admonished himself. Pretending to capsize the dinghy accidentally! And then being stupid enough to hit his head. He hadn't meant to be so violent about it—Lord, what if it had been Stacy who had been hurt?

"Mmmm." She sighed and snuggled against him, caressing his nipple. The tiny point grew taut and sensitive. Keith pressed his thighs together in an ache of want and took a slow, deep breath. Of course, if she'd been hurt, he would've towed the dinghy himself, gripping the line as he swam. It would be easy for him to make the journey. After all, he had been a lifeguard for five years at one of the world's busiest beaches. Besides, he still spent more time swimming and surfing than anything else.

Well, just about anything else . . .

Stacy stirred. He looked down to find her star-
tlingly green eyes half-opened, a look of confusion
on her face.

"I'm so *hot*," she murmured.

He groaned silently. This *menehune* was aroused,
and too drunk to realize it.

"I feel like I'm burning up."

He pressed the bridge of his nose. "Ah, it'll pass. It
happens. I feel the same way."

"You do?" When he nodded, she closed her eyes
and rested her head back against his chest.

He nearly leaped out of his skin when her hand
fell into his lap, covering his manhood, which strained
inside his clothes. *Wake up, wake up,* he implored
her. Instead she began to snore.

Keith swallowed hard and leaned his head against
a rock. "I know I deserve it," he said to the black roof
of the cave. "I know it."

Later, when she shifted herself so that her head
lay in his lap, tears actually formed in his eyes.

Like the day before, Stacy awakened squinting as
bright sunlight streamed down on her. Before she
opened her eyes, she had a flash of a thought—the
motel was costing her a fortune and she wasn't even
using it! Then she sat up quickly, grabbed her pounding head, and sank back down on stiff, ungiving
wood.

"*Aloha kakahiaka,*" Keith said pleasantly. He was
sitting above her in the dinghy, rowing at a leisurely
pace. "Good morning."

She stared up at him. She was lying on the bottom of the boat, her panty hose and sandals arranged beside her hand. Otherwise, she was clothed
in her green dress, which was completely dry.

"How did I get here?" she asked him, though of
course the answer was obvious.

"The *menehunes* did it," he replied. "They pushed
the oars to shore, too. When I woke up, I grabbed

them and flipped the boat over—with their help, of course. And then they carried you into the boat. Oh, and a very nice lady *menehune* took off your shoes and stockings." He sighed. "I wanted to do it, but she wouldn't let me."

In spite of herself, Stacy smiled weakly. "What a nice lady."

"Yes, she was." As he loomed above her, she was struck again by the blueness of his eyes. They matched the bright, brilliant sky behind his head, and his hair was like blinding sunshine shot with moonbeams. His chest and arms, tanned and bare, rippled with the strength of mountains. His thighs were wide apart, and though he had tucked the ends of the batiked fabric of his lava-lava between his legs, she could still see flashes of his white underwear and the shape of the fullness inside them.

Unsteadily she sat up, which brought her eye-level with his pelvis, and she scooted back on her bottom in an attempt to climb onto the seat facing him. But her arms were like rubber. Her wild night of debauchery had zapped her energy.

"Too much champagne," she muttered.

"I shouldn't have let you drink so much," he said apologetically.

" 'Let' me? You practically forced it down my throat."

"Only at first. But then you got grabby."

"I . . . did?" she asked in a small voice. She ran a hand through her hair. "I don't remember anything." She hung her head. "I'm so embarrassed. I don't usually act like this, you know. I hardly ever drink, maybe a glass of wine . . ."

He smiled. "Take it easy. You didn't do anything you shouldn't have."

"A term subject to varying definitions," she said, sighing. "What I think I shouldn't do and what you think I shouldn't do are probably totally opposite things."

His smile broadened. "I was using your definition. Nothing happened, Stacy."

She swallowed. "Except you took off my panty hose."

He shook his head. "The *menehune* lady did that. I told you." He grew serious. "I'm not the kind of guy to take advantage of a woman in a situation like that, *ipo*. Believe me." He stuck out his chest in a self-deprecating gesture of bravado. "I don't usually need to."

Her unease made her defensive. "Are you trying to imply that there's something wrong with me because I haven't yet fallen at your feet?"

"No, not at all," he hastened to assure her. He cocked his head, a curious, bemused look on his face as he studied her. "In fact, something is telling me that there's something very right about the way our relationship is progressing."

"We—we don't have a relationship." She took a deep breath and cupped her elbows in her hands. She really couldn't remember anything!

Keith let go of one of the oars and touched her cheek. "Sure, we do, *malihini*," he said tenderly.

Five

Keith rowed back to his grandmother's, then practically dragged Stacy to the house. She hung back, humiliated by her appearance and by what Tutu Ewa might think—that she had spent the night with Keith, like some promiscuous beach bunny from California or something. But Keith insisted that his grandmother wouldn't judge her.

"Besides, you need a decent breakfast. You must be starving." He encircled her wrist with his thumb and forefinger. "Look at that. Skin and bones!"

Finally she followed him into the house, to be greeted warmly by both Tutu Ewa and Olga. At the sight of the two wanderers, Olga gave an anguished cry and raced into Stacy's arms, nearly bowling her smaller friend over.

"Olga, I'm sorry," Stacy said at once. "I knew you would worry. The boat tipped over and we had to spend the night in the cave because we couldn't find the oars, and—" Her eyes widened. "Keith, how's your head? Tutu, he might need to go to the hospital."

"Anastasia, shut upsky, please!" Olga cut in. "I am having spasm attack because of KGB!"

Stacy looked at Olga. The woman was pale, and

her brown eyes were glittering with unshed tears. "What?"

"They are here! I listen in darkness. I am hearing them by door, lurching."

"Lurking," Stacy corrected her. She gave Olga a big hug. "Olgavitch, you know we've talked about this. The KGB isn't after you anymore. You're safe in America."

Olga frowned. "I am forgetting Hawaii is part of U.S.A." She squirmed. "I am insulting Tutu."

"So you've met," Keith said, kissing his grandmother's cheek. "Good morning. Hope we didn't worry you."

Tutu Ewa gave him a wry look. "No, Kika. I didn't worry." She gestured to Olga. "Kapono brought her over. She called from the motel a few hours ago."

"I am waking up everybody," Olga said miserably. "I feel like most big idiot in Western world."

"Well, don't," Keith said, giving her a squeeze. "Listen, everybody take a seat for a minute and I'll make breakfast. Tutu, Stacy might like a shower."

Stacy felt ashamed in front of the elderly lady. Tutu Ewa must be convinced they'd slept together, she thought. "I—I fell," she murmured.

"We'll fix you up in no time." Tutu smiled at her and led the way to a shower. "I can lend you a muumuu to wear while I wash your dress." She laughed over her shoulder. "Didn't we just do this before? By the way, Kika, your jeans are dry."

"*Mahalo*," Keith called. "I'll put them on as soon as I make breakfast."

"I am helping?" Olga asked.

"Sure. I'll bet you're a whiz at cracking eggs."

"With one hand only," she said proudly.

The back screen door slid open and Kapono stepped into the room. "Olga?" he called. When he saw her, his eyes gleamed. "There you are."

"We are cracking eggs," Olga announced, indicating that Kapono should follow her into the kitchen.

"Your friend's made quite a conquest," Tutu Ewa said in the same mischievous tone Stacy had heard

Keith use. "I never thought either of those boys would get serious about anything or anybody, but . . ." Grinning at Stacy, she left the rest unsaid.

Once the omelettes were started, Olga excused herself to visit with Stacy while Stacy dressed in Tutu Ewa's bathroom. Tutu left to make sure Lani's kittens were nursing properly. And, so, Keith was alone with his cousin as he cooked the bacon in Tutu's cast-iron frying pan.

"Honest, Kapono, I didn't touch her," Keith insisted. "She was so tired, and we had a lot of champagne."

"Exactly the right time to go for it, bruddah." Kapono scratched his head. "I don't get it. I mean, she is one gorgeous lady, and you had a chance, man."

Keith scowled at Kapono. "I won't talk about her like this. It's insulting to her."

Kapono groaned. "Oh, no, Kika. Don't do this."

"Do what?"

"Don't . . . fall for her. I knew she was trouble when she walked into the restaurant! I could see it even then."

Keith rolled his eyes. "Kapono, that's a lot of nonsense. You didn't see any such thing." He busied himself with turning the bacon and popping a heap of toast into the oven to keep it warm. "And while we're on the subject of women, what about Olga? I saw the way you lit up when you saw her."

Kapono chuckled. "She's a big *wahine*, isn't she?"

"Maybe too big for you, friend. If you mess with her she'll probably break your arm."

"I'm keeping my cool, Kika. Unlike some stupid islanders I know."

Keith looked at Kapono sideways. "I'm keeping my cool."

"Yeah, right. You're sizzling hotter than that bacon, cousin."

"I am not!"

Kapono held out his arms. "Hey, man, we're fighting. We never fight. Not even when Uncle Ray left us the restaurant and I wanted to sell it. Let's call a truce, okay? After breakfast, let's drop off the girls and go surfing."

Keith made a moue of apology. "I'm sorry, Kapono. I told Stacy I'd help her with the treasure hunt." Argh, a lie to his best friend in the world! Maybe Kapono was right—maybe he was getting too involved. But how could he know how involved was *too* involved? He didn't have much experience in developing a relationship with a woman. He had always been too busy playing the field.

Because of Dad, a little voice whispered, but he ignored it and checked the bacon again.

"Oh, Kika," Kapono said mournfully. "You got it, bruddah, and you got it bad."

Keith wiped his hands on his apron and faced his cousin. "What? What have I got?"

Kapono shrugged. "If you don't know, I'm not telling you."

Behind them in the doorway, Tutu Ewa smiled and continued to eavesdrop on her two favorite grandchildren. She didn't feel a bit guilty doing it. As the matriarch, it was her duty to know what was going on with all the members of her family.

Could it be, Kika in love at last? She fervently hoped so.

Quickly, before they could realize she'd been standing there, she glided into the kitchen and put her arms around her two sturdy grandsons.

"Is it almost ready? We womenfolk are hungry. I put Stacy in one of your mother's muumuus. My, she's small!"

"So is dynamite," Kapono grumbled, "but it can blow you up just the same."

Tutu stood on tiptoe and kissed Kapono's cheek. "And that Olga! So clever and strong."

"Yeah," Keith said, staring accusingly at Kapono. "What do you have to say about Olga, bruddah?"

"It's not like you and Stacy," Kapono said.

"What's not like him and Stacy?" Tutu Ewa asked. Oh, could *both* of them be falling in love? Better and better!

"Nothing, Tutu." Kapono's brown cheeks turned pink, making them look like baked luau apples.

"Breakfast is ready," Keith said. "I'll set the table."

Tutu laid a gentle hand on his arm. "I already did it." Her eyes danced with anticipation. "Everything's ready, my beautiful boys. Everything's in place."

After breakfast, Stacy and Olga washed the dishes while Keith and Kapono pulled out matching guitars and played together. The men's fingers were nimble, and they raced each other during the fast pieces, then strummed in harmony for the slow ones. They sang Hawaiian folk songs in deep, resonant voices that sent chills up Stacy's spine.

Olga was affected too. "Sound like Russian baby songs," she said as she handed Stacy a spatula to dry.

"Lullabies?" Stacy asked.

"Exactly. Anastasia, you are having ESP. And I am having same with you. You like our hot boy, *da*?"

Before Stacy could answer, Keith put down his guitar and sauntered into the kitchen. He had changed back into his jeans, and as he leaned against the door jamb, Stacy had a flash of memory. Had she . . . *caressed* him in some way last night? Her fingertips retained a distinct impression of hard chest muscles and crisp blond hair. Oh, good heavens, what had she done?

"How would you ladies like a tour of the island today?" he asked, glancing at his cousin, who sputtered but said nothing.

"Oh, that is best idea in Western world," Olga said at the same time that Stacy replied, "Thanks, but I have some reading to do. And we'll need to find out where we can rent a boat." She frowned. "And a car, too, I guess. We certainly can't walk to the boat from that motel."

"Is not good place," Olga said, shivering.

Keith regarded Stacy. "You're going to read all day? *Here*?"

She raised her chin. "Don't you ever read?"

Apparently he didn't realize he was being insulted. "Of course, but I live here. I can see the Na Pali Coast and Lumahai Beach and the fern grotto and Wailua Falls anytime I want. And Spouting Horn and the Hanapepe River and—"

"Anastasia!" Olga wailed. "We are missing this for statistical analysis?"

"I can help with that," Kapono said, coming up behind Keith. "I keep the books for the restaurant."

Olga looked at him askance. "You are knowing of chi square and other such terms?"

He shrugged. "I catch on fast."

"Maybe we should just rest on the beach for a while," Keith cut in, perhaps sensing that Kapono was losing ground for him. "Stacy hasn't had much sleep."

As one person, Kapono and Olga looked at Stacy questioningly. She felt conspicuous in Nele's lovely blue floor-length muumuu, a pale tourist in costume, something of a fraud. She tried, unsuccessfully, to keep from blushing, and made a great show of drying Tutu's heavy skillet.

What had she done? she wondered, anguished.

"Jet lag can kill you if you're not careful," Keith went on. "Why don't you nap this morning, then we'll sightsee, and you can study tonight?"

Warning bells went off in Stacy's brain. She hadn't come to Kauai to have an island romance. She had come for serious research. She had a lot to accomplish before the fish were due, and she couldn't afford to be distracted.

She couldn't afford to fall in love, a little voice piped up. Not with him, anyway. He wasn't at all her type. Someday she would meet and need a fellow intellectual, not some muscular hunk who thought reading was what you did when there wasn't anything else to do.

But he hadn't said that, another voice noted in his defense. He hadn't said he didn't read.

"I think that frying pan's as dry as it's going to get," Keith said.

Stacy looked down to see that she was rubbing the same spot over and over, and put the skillet back on the stove.

"I guess I'm tireder than I realized. I'd better go back to the motel for a while."

Olga made a face. "Not to that place, I am begging, Anastasia. It creeps me."

"You can sack out under some palm trees and start work on your tan," Keith said. "But you'll have to put some of Tutu's lotion on, or you'll wind up with first-degree burns. The sun here is fierce."

So was his persistence, Stacy thought, folding the dish towel and laying it on the counter. Suddenly she was so exhausted, she couldn't think anymore. He was persistent and he was right. She needed a nap.

"Okay, I give in. But I'm not so sure falling asleep on the beach is a great idea. I want to go back to the motel."

Olga started to protest, but Keith replied, "Okay. The motel it is."

After saying good-bye to Tutu, they left in two cars, Stacy and Keith in his Jeep, Kapono close behind in a rattling old T-Bird that had once belonged to their Uncle Ray.

"The same uncle who willed Baggies to us," Keith explained as they pulled in front of the motel. "It used to be a real ramshackle place. Its only claim to fame was mango jelly." He smiled. "After we hired all my lifeguard buddies, it became a tourist spot."

"Yes, I know," Stacy said, stepping from the Jeep as Keith held open the door. "I read about it in the guidebook."

"You really did your homework before you came

here, didn't you?" he said, lacing his fingers through hers.

"I always do my homework."

"But there are some things you can't prepare for, Stacy. Some things you can't learn about in books."

"Like getting a tan?" she asked archly.

"Hmm. I'm beginning to get the distinct impression you don't approve of me."

She was abashed. "Well, I—"

"But you still like me," he said confidently. "That's what really counts."

Was it? she wondered. Before her arrival on Kauai, she had been obsessed with the prospect of finding the Pele's Fire. And now?

"I am still much jet-logged as well," she heard Olga saying as the four of them walked down a wooden corridor and Stacy pulled out the key. "But I am preferring to suntan on beach. I am dressing in my suit and meeting with you, Kaponovitch?"

"Sure." Kapono flashed a triumphant smile at Keith and said something to him in Hawaiian. "Tell you what," he went on in English. "There's a super place a few miles down the coast. We'll drive there in the T-Bird."

"That is good. Anastasia can therefore sleep alone." Olga looked flustered. "I mean, without disturbance."

Stacy could feel Keith gazing at her, waiting for her response to the news that Olga would be leaving her unchaperoned. She said nothing, only opened the door and led the way into the small room. With four people standing in it, it was crowded, and Keith's arm brushed against hers as she made room for Olga to fetch her suitcase.

In no time at all, Olga had changed in the bathroom, pulled on a knit shirt and jeans over her suit, and grabbed up her sandals and purse.

"I am back in a few whiles," she told Stacy. "Get good sleep." Her lids flickered as she nodded to Keith. "*Do svidániya.* Take it easy."

"Aloha. See you, cousin," Keith said to Kapono.

Too soon the door closed and Stacy and Keith were alone.

They looked at each other. "Well," Stacy said.

"Here we are."

Had she touched him last night? she wondered again. Had they kissed? She straightened a stack of books on the nightstand, lined up a pencil and a ruler, and slipped her calculator back into its vinyl case. She sensed that Keith hadn't moved, but stood watching her. His gaze on her back was like a candle flame held too close—not enough to cause injury, but too warm for comfort.

"Stacy . . ."

"I'm tired," she said quickly. "I need to sleep." She thought about pulling back the bedspread to make a point, but then thought better of it. She didn't even want to acknowledge the presence of the bed while he was in the room.

"Stacy . . ."

She couldn't believe she was behaving like this. Good grief, she was a grown woman working on her Ph.D., not some eighteen-year-old let loose for her first vacation on her own. She knew how to conduct herself around strange men.

But what had she *done* last night?

Keith was right. There *were* some things you couldn't learn in books. And she hadn't learned how to deal with a man, not really, nor how to handle the wild, soaring responses Keith's attentions elicited in her.

"Please, I'm tired," she said again, more clearly, and whirled around to face him.

But he was gone.

"Oh," she cried, startled . . . and more than a little disappointed.

She shook her head. "Good grief," she muttered. "I don't believe this. All I wanted to do was find my fish and get back to Michigan."

And now?

"I'm tired," she said aloud to drown out the unspoken answer to the question.

But after she crawled beneath the sheets, carefully draping Nele's muumuu over the foot of the bed, her heart whispered, *Now Keith*.

When she woke up, Keith was standing by the bed.

Her heart soared even as she indignantly yanked the sheets to her neck. Though she was still wearing her bra and panties, she felt naked. Her voice was high-pitched and nervous as she asked, "How long have you been standing there?"

Causing her mingled dread and anticipation, he sat on the bed and took her hand. "I told you, *mali-hini*, there's no sense of time here."

"Can't you just answer a simple question?"

He smiled gently. "Don't be nervous."

"I'm not nervous. Why should I be nervous?"

"You have roses in your cheeks," he said, trailing a finger from her temple to the hollow beneath her cheekbone. "You're a peaches-and-cream girl. It makes me want to push the sun farther away so it won't burn you."

"I'm not nervous."

But she stiffened when he bent forward to kiss her forehead. "I know, Stacy. I know." He sat back and studied her. "I like your hair down," he said, smoothing her tangled curls over the sheet.

"Olga and Kapono are back," he went on. "I saw the T-bird pulling up a minute ago."

She was startled. "Have you been here all day?"

He nodded. "I went for a walk on the beach."

"All day?"

"However long you've been asleep. I just came in the door a moment ago."

"Oh." She stared at his brown fingers resting on her hair and took a deep breath. "Keith, you must be honest with me. What happened last night?"

He wound a tendril of her hair around his finger and caressed it with his thumb. "Stacy, if we'd made love, don't you think you'd be able to tell?"

His frank answer embarrassed her, partly because she wasn't sure. She had led such a manless existence for so long that she honestly couldn't recall the morning-after sensations of lovemaking.

"But I know something happened," she whispered, not quite able to look at him. "Somehow, I know things about you I didn't know before."

"Well, yes, a few things happened."

Her eyes widened. A muscle jumped in Keith's cheek and his Adam's apple bobbed with a deep swallow.

Her eyes grew wider. "Why are you reacting like that?"

"Because when you look at me with those emerald eyes, I burn. And melt. I can hardly control myself. Like last night . . ."

She pressed her back against the headboard. "Like last night?" she echoed. "What did you do to me last night?"

Instead of defending himself, which she expected him to do, he laughed. "Unfortunately, not much. To be honest, most of the doing was done by *you*."

"Me?" she asked in a tiny voice.

"You."

"What . . . what did I do?"

His features softened. His eyes became hooded beneath the heavy fringes of brown-sugar lashes and his golden skin seemed to glow.

"This," he murmured, drawing the sheet away from her chest. She gasped, but he bunched the sheet around her waist and fanned his hand over her shoulder and collarbone.

"And this." Slowly, implacably, his hand glided downward and cupped her breast.

She started. At once she was awash with intense pleasure, her gaze riveted to his, and her whole being seemed to vibrate to an unsung song, a powerful *kahuna* chant of desire that emanated from his broad chest as it rose and fell in time with hers. There was magic in the room, powerful magic in his fingers, his look, the very breath he exhaled. It prevented her from moving. She sat as still as a statue, inundated with the joy of his hand on her body—at last! at last!

The sensations were so fierce, they were almost painful. It was as if his fingers were white-hot, burning through her filmy white bra. But she was powerless to stop him as he fondled her soft roundness with silky caresses, his thumb rubbing the awakening bud of her nipple.

"Nnn . . ." She tried to speak, to grab his hand and force him to stop, but his blue eyes held her as he moved to her other breast. Her flesh swelled and grew in his strong grasp. Her body sizzled from her neck to the moist heat between her thighs, and she felt herself quickening there, wanting him, insisting on having him.

"You touched me last night," he whispered. "I wanted you, oh, how I wanted you, but I knew it wasn't the time. But Stacy, for us this is a time. A time to touch each other like this." He ran the tips of his fingers inside her bra, exploring her white smoothness, nearly grazing the twin circles of rosy pink.

"And like this." He began to slip the bra strap off her right shoulder. When it looped around her upper arm, he kissed the light line it had left. His hair was soft as fur when it brushed her neck and chest.

"And like this," he said, fastening his lips around her taut red nipple

"Ah." Stacy gasped aloud, finally able to move. She clutched his head, her fingers burying themselves in his thick hair, as if to hold him to her breast forever.

Shooting stars went off inside her. *Yes, now!* she wanted to cry. *Now, everything!*

But then there was noise in the hall.

Keith moaned. "They're here."

Stacy blinked dizzily. "Who?" she asked, and then reality flooded back in around her. Olga and Kapono, of course! And they would be in here any second!

There was a tentative knock on the door.

"Anastasia?"

"Quick, hurry," Stacy murmured as Keith helped her with the shoulder strap.

He caught her chin between his thumb and forefinger. "Don't be so guilty, Emerald Eyes. We weren't doing anything we shouldn't."

"The muumuu, please," she said tightly. He handed it to her and she drew it over her head. Unsteadily she climbed out of bed.

"Stacy, it's all right," Keith said once more.

"Anastasia?" Olga called a little more loudly. Then, in a softer tone, "Perhaps we must come back later."

"No, it's okay," Stacy said, smoothing her hair. "Come on in."

"We're not finished, you know that," Keith said in an undervoice as the door opened. He lifted her hand to his lips and kissed her wrist, where her pulse throbbed violently. "Now that we've tasted each other, neither of us will be satisfied until we have each other."

How could a universe exist in one pair of blue eyes? she wondered. "You're wrong."

"You know I'm not. You know—"

"Aloha," Olga said, breezing into the room. She was wearing a shocking-pink muumuu topped with a huge white carnation lei. Its mate hung around Kapono's neck. "You have good nap?"

"Yes."

"Good. We are doing many fun things. We have made suntan and gone to purchase many small souvenirs." She gestured to the immense sack she carried. "Look what I am buying for you, Anastasia!" Proudly she pulled out a book entitled *Hawaiian First Names.*

"Thank you," Stacy said, bemused by her gift. It was an odd choice, she thought. A book of names—for what?

And then her mouth dropped open. Only last week she and Olga had attended a baby shower for one of the professors' wives. The joke of the party was that the lady received not one, not two, but three books of names for the baby.

The baby! Stacy made a face at Olga, who ignored her. "And for you, fish book," she said, handing Keith a weighty tome. "So you and Anastasia are having many interesting discussions."

The corners of Keith's mouth twitched. "*Mahalo*, Olga."

"Means 'thank you,' " Olga informed Stacy. "Now we are seesighting, *da*? All four?" For the first time, she really looked at Stacy. Her eyes glittered as she took in her friend's disheveled appearance. "Unless you are doing other things?"

"We'd love to go sightseeing," Stacy said quickly, then realized she'd bamboozled herself into going after all. She'd entertained the idea of staying behind to work on her statistical analysis. Instead she'd just betrayed herself into spending more time with Keith.

The very thought made her clammy with unease . . . and warm with expectation. Her breasts were still vibrating from his caresses, her wrist aflame from his kiss . . . and her mind was trying desperately to remember that she was here to do research, not to experiment with fire.

"Good," Olga said. "Kaponovitch has suggested we are merely driving, to see many fine wonders along road."

"Spouting Horn and all that," Kapono said to Keith. "We can stop to eat along the way."

"Just a minute," Stacy interjected. "We can't stay out too long. I have work to do."

The cousins traded looks. "Anastasia, is only one day!" Olga said petulantly.

"We'll help you tomorrow," Keith added. "We'll do whatever you need us to."

She frowned. "Don't you two have a restaurant to run?"

Keith shrugged. "Only when we feel like it. The boys will take care of everything, more or less." He flashed a winning smile at Stacy. "What's more important, a few grilled fish or a night with two lovely *malihinis*?"

"But your responsibilities . . ."

He theatrically shielded himself. "Another one of those *kapu* words."

"When we decided to keep the restaurant, we agreed it would never rule our lives," Kapono said. "We're Mo'okinis, not mainland businessmen."

"So we are going!" Olga said, setting down her sack.

Stacy could see she was outnumbered. She was also depressed by what Keith and Kapono had said— how they had boasted that they didn't believe in responsibility. That was the exact opposite of every ideal she held dear. To her, life was based on upholding your obligations, fulfilling your goals, having a purpose . . . and these two thought no further than having a good time.

"Anastasia?"

"All right. But tomorrow things are going to change," she said firmly.

Keith brushed her hand. "Oh, yes, Emerald Eyes," he said quietly, so that only she could hear him. "I certainly hope so."

Keith loved showing Stacy the wonders of his island. He loved the way she inhaled sharply when the sun sparkled on the waves as Kapono's old T-bird wound its way on Highway 50, high above the sea. He loved it when she giggled at the flume of water spraying from Spouting Horn.

"Look at the rainbow in it!" she cried when the flume hovered in the air, then crashed down on the lava rocks.

"Yes," he said, putting his arm around her shoulders, rejoicing when she didn't move away.

She loved Poipu Beach, and Nawiliwili Harbor, and could easily see the silhouette of the Sleeping Giant as he reclined on the volcanic mountains.

Keith loved their afternoon together. And when night

fell and she didn't say a word about getting to work, he loved that too.

Love. As he sat beside her in the little Japanese restaurant run by one of his friends, he wondered if the soaring sensation he felt could be the beginning of love.

No way, he thought. No way!

He shook himself and picked up his mai tai, only to see his cousin glowering at him. He shrugged in response and leaned back in his chair.

Just then Olga, who had gone to the rest room, charged back to the table. "Owner of this place has Russian daughter-in-law! He asks if I am liking to meet her."

"How nice," Stacy said. "Why don't you?"

"Okay. Kaponovitch, you are coming?"

Kapono glanced at his cousin, and Keith knew he was caught in a bind. He wanted to court Olga, but he didn't like leaving Keith with Stacy.

"Go ahead," Keith said lazily. "We'll be fine."

"You don't mind?" Olga asked Stacy.

"Not a bit."

"Good. The man says he will drive us back later. Kapono, you give car keys to Keith and we go."

Stacy paled. "You mean you're going away for a long time?"

"*Da.* Many hours. Have good evening!" She sailed away before Stacy could respond.

Bless her soul, Keith thought. He understood that she was giving him the second opportunity of the day to be alone with her adored Anastasia.

After handing his keys to Keith with a warning glance, Kapono trailed after her. The two disappeared into the kitchen.

"I think they're hitting it off," Keith said.

Stacy was staring down at her iced tea. "Oh, Olga likes him, but I don't think it goes much further than that."

"You don't? How can you tell?"

"We're best friends. I'd know if Olga was really crazy about a guy."

He looked at Stacy thoughtfully. He could tell she felt his gaze on her but was trying to ignore it. His heart went out to her—she was so darned nervous around him!—but that didn't stop him from pursuing her. Or from gazing at her. She was incredibly beautiful.

"Would you know if *you* were really crazy about a guy?" he asked.

She looked at him warily. "What do you mean?"

Come to think of it, would he know it if he were really crazy about a woman? he wondered. It had never been an issue before.

"I don't know what I mean," he said honestly, then laughed at himself. "I'm just a beachboy, what do I know?"

Oh, she glowed. In the soft light from the paper lanterns, she glowed. He wanted to put his hands near her face and capture the light radiating from it.

"Remember how I chanted when I took you to Tutu's?" he asked, holding her hand. "That was a love chant."

"How . . . interesting."

"It has a lot of power in it." Beneath his breath, he began the rhythmic incantation. He felt her hand involuntarily squeeze his, her pupils dilating.

He sang and she listened, mesmerized. Yes, there was power in the old ways, he thought. Just as there was power in the hold she had over him . . . though she didn't even know it.

"Come on," he said hoarsely, breaking off the chant. If he finished and they fell in love . . . what then?

"Where are we going?"

"To a special place. Come." He spoke the word like a command.

He expected her to refuse or at least to ask more questions, but she surprised him. Without speaking, she waited as he paid for their meal, then followed him out the door.

They climbed into the car and drove. Then they walked, and the first sound between them was her gasp as they came upon a ravine filled with a waterfall.

It was the most magical place he knew. The waterfall leaped off the rocks high above, and thousands of flowers grew at its base. Behind it there was a sheltered alcove laden with plumeria blossoms.

"This is a *heiau*," he said. After so long a silence his voice sounded too loud. "A sacred altar, where the old Hawaiians worshiped their gods."

They stood together. He could feel her warmth beside him, and suddenly he could bear it no longer. He turned to her and gathered her into his arms. She resisted for only a moment.

"Keith . . ." Her lips trembled.

Auwe, he thought, her breasts were soft, her heart fluttering like a captive bird. His body responded at once, burning and chilling at the same time, and he felt the energy of the waterfall rushing into his manhood.

"This *heiau* is where I will worship you, Stacy." His voice shook as he looked into her emerald eyes. She was his. He knew it and exulted in the knowledge.

"Now is the moment."

Six

Stacy stared into Keith's eyes. They were going to make love here, now, and there was nothing she could do—or wanted to do—to prevent it.

"I don't understand," she whispered, thrilling as his lids drooped and he smiled gently at her, his face rosy with ardor. "I wasn't going to . . ."

"I think the *heiau* worked its magic on you." He leaned toward her and she closed her eyes, thinking he would kiss her. But he smoothed her hair away from her forehead and molded the side of her face with his hand.

"Stacy, lovely Stacy. My *wahine*," he murmured, his hand warm and strong, his long fingers stroking her hairline.

No, *he* had worked his magic on her, she thought dizzily, each nerve in her body attuned to the places he was touching. Like the sea, he had worn away her resistance, until there was nothing left but the desire that lay hidden beneath the protective barrier. All washed away, all exposed, by his patient but firm insistence.

She opened her eyes, feeling the moisture in them. For her the moment was bittersweet. She suspected

that once she made love to him, she would be like all
the other women who passed through his bachelor
existence.

"You've won," she said throatily. "You're a master
at this, Keith. I should've known I wouldn't be able
to hold out against you."

He looked troubled. "Stacy . . ."

"And now you'll think I'm . . . easy."

"Don't—be silly."

"Oh, I know I sound old-fashioned, but—"

"Ssh, don't be afraid." He pressed his lips reverently where his fingers had caressed her. "I won't
hurt you. I would never hurt you."

Her voice was shaky. "I'm not afraid."

"There's no need. You know I respect you now
and I'll respect you afterward. You know that. You
know me."

Eyes like the sea, she mused. She thought then he
would kiss her, but still he didn't. Instead he put
one arm around her back and the other under her
knees and swept her up against his chest. His arm
muscles flexed, hard as stone against her soft, yield-
ing form.

The rush of the waterfall grew louder as he walked
down a trail cut into a forest of ferns and vines,
never taking his gaze off her. Her muumuu hung
over her feet and draped across his lower body like a
billowing net filled with dark blue flowers that
matched the color of the night sky. She wore nothing beneath it but her bra and panties, and she
could feel the indentation of each of his fingers
through the thin fabric. Soon there would be no
clothes at all, and his hands would stroke her bare
skin, and then . . .

The moon gauzed his gold-and-silver hair as he
moved easily down the path, not losing stride even
on the sharp incline that angled toward the waterfall. Stacy, not speaking, clung to his neck and tried,
for one last time, to summon the power to prevent
the inevitable.

But it was too late for that. It had been too late the

"alluring"..."inspiring"...
"irresistible"...

Loveswept

EXAMINE 4 LOVESWEPT NOVELS FOR

15 Days FREE!

Turn page for details

America's most popular, most compelling romance novels...

Loveswept

Here, at last...love stories that really involve you! Fresh, finely crafted novels with story lines so believable you'll feel you're actually living them!

Read a Loveswept novel and you'll experience all the very real feelings of two people as they discover and build an involved relationship: laughing, crying, learning and loving. Characters you can relate to... exciting places to visit...unexpected plot twists...all in all, exciting romances that satisfy your mind and delight your heart.

And now you can be sure you'll never, ever miss a single Loveswept title by enrolling in our special reader's home delivery service. A service that will bring all four new Loveswept romances published every month into your home—and deliver them to you *before* they appear in the bookstores!

Examine 4 Loveswept Novels for

15 Days FREE!

To introduce you to this fabulous service, you'll get four brand-new Loveswept releases not yet in the bookstores. These four exciting new titles are yours to examine for 15 days without obligation to buy. Keep them if you wish for just $9.95 plus postage and handling and any applicable sales tax.

SEND NO MONEY NOW.
RETURN THIS
POSTAGE-PAID CARD TODAY!

first time Keith had focused those brilliant blue eyes on her, when he had flashed her his mischievous, bad-boy grin. When he had taken her hand and said, "Come," leading her into his breathtaking plumeria orchard—and into a world she had never known before, far beyond the walls of libraries and research halls. Far, far beyond . . .

They were near the bottom of the path when Keith stopped and looked up at the moon. Stacy did the same, leaning her head against his chest. She inhaled his tangy coconut scent, a hint of musk, pure masculine essence.

"Ah," he whispered, and kissed her temple. Then he pressed his chin against her hair and nuzzled her in an affectionate gesture that moved her in a way none of his more erotic attentions ever had. Oh, he was kind, he was dear, he would never, never cause her pain. . . .

"No," she gasped, coming at last to her senses. She blinked as if she were awakening from a heavy sleep. Had that chant really bewitched her? Was she crazy?

She struggled to free herself. "No. Put me down. I have work to do. . . . I can't stay here any longer."

"Ssh, don't be afraid," he repeated in his gentle voice. "I realize you haven't been with a man in a long time."

His words mortified her. "How can you know that? We're strangers to each other! You say I know you. We don't know anything about each other. You don't even know the reason I came to Kauai. You—you think I'm a *treasure hunter*, for heaven's sake!"

"Hush, dear."

"Stop saying that!" She wriggled in his grasp, but he held her tightly. His strength was too much for her. Unless he deigned to let her go, she would have to remain in his arms.

"Keith," she pleaded.

He continued walking toward the waterfall. "If you really wanted to leave, I would let you. But you're wrong, Stacy. I *do* know you, and I know that deep in your soul you don't wish to go. And I know the real reason you're on Kauai."

"You . . . do?"

"Yes. You came here to be with me. I know that now. I know it."

He started to chant again, the compelling rhythms sounding beneath the cascade of crystal water. She turned her head, trying not to listen. She was beginning to believe that perhaps there really was some magic in the ancient song . . . and in his eyes. Perhaps the supernatural aided Keith in his conquest of women.

Perhaps he himself was supernatural.

Oh, but she was being foolish. He was just a man.

And yet her fear—for, yes, he was right, she was afraid, terribly afraid—began to slide away again. And as it dissolved, the warm desire that had faintly glowed during her remorse and doubt grew hotter. Heat prickled along the tops of her legs to her abdomen, her breasts, the moist place between her thighs.

He reached the banks of the waterfall and looked down on her.

"Truly, you're a most beautiful woman. You're like the first woman, and I'm the first man. And here we are together, innocent, in paradise."

"Innocent?" she breathed.

His breath was warm on her neck and cheek. "Innocent of bad intentions, and cruelty, and deception. You know what I am, Stacy. And I know what you are. There will be no guilt between us over what we do tonight."

"But . . ." She understood what he was trying to say, but he was wrong. She knew what she believed about sex, that it entailed more than a physical act. It was an emotional one as well—or should be. Keith wouldn't feel guilty because he had no expectations about what lovemaking brought with it. But once she gave herself to him, she would have tasted the apple. She would be capable of being hurt by him, because she would care for him far too much.

"You think you know me, but you don't," she said

unsteadily. "You don't understand that if we make love—"

"Hush, *ipo*. Hush."

Quickly he carried her along the bank to the underside of the waterfall. Plumeria trees had dropped their petals on the earth there, and a carpet a foot thick sent up its heady fragrance as Keith walked through it.

Then carefully, lovingly, he lay Stacy on the mattress of petals. She sank into the blossoms, and their scent filled her as she inhaled.

Keith lowered himself carefully on top of her, supporting his weight on his elbows. He covered the top of her head with his hands, then combed her hair with his fingers as he drew a shaky breath.

"So beautiful," he murmured, and then he kissed her.

He was gentle at first. His lips were as soft as the plumeria petals, velvet rolling over her mouth, dry and tasting of the sweet mai tai he'd had at dinner. He trailed his mouth to her cheeks, sliding along her jaw to the sensitive flesh of her earlobe.

When he exhaled, the entire side of her body tingled. Digging into the petals, he cupped her neck and head and cradled them. He moved her head as he pleased, kissing her behind her ear and down the back of her neck.

She arched slightly, not able to quell her response as more chills jolted through her. She felt as if she were falling off a cliff. There was no way to stop her descent, yet he would hold her all the way down so that she wouldn't be injured. He was holding her, and protecting her, and loving her. . . .

Oh, but he *wasn't* loving her! He didn't love her!

"Let go of everything," Keith said, breaking her train of thought. "Stop the mental churning. Feel what I have to give you. Feel *me*."

"I can't."

"Yes, yes, you can, Stacy Livingston. Just let go for an hour. Stop fretting and worrying and analyzing and enjoy me. I'm here to please you."

"I'm too uptight." She gave a nervous laugh. "You've said so yourself."

"Then I'll make you stop thinking," he said, and bruised her mouth with his.

He let his full weight crush against her as he held her captive beneath him, grinding his body against hers. Stacy felt the searing hot length of him, the fullness of his manhood, and bucked beneath him. His arms were like iron and his body was steel, and she finally had to open her mouth to breathe.

And when she did, he slid his tongue between her lips. He explored the secret, sensitive places of her mouth and sought her tongue. He dueled and probed, demanding a response from her. She fought against it, tried to remember that this was all a mistake, that it had been the chanting that had made her forget that she mustn't, shouldn't, give in to him.

But then she *was* responding. She was clinging to him, her arms wrapped around his shoulders, and her kiss was as fierce as his. She was on fire, barely able to think. Every part of her wanted him, craved him, clung to him.

"Yes," he whispered, breaking the kiss to brand the skin beneath her chin and burn a trail to the hollow at the base of her throat. "Yes, my Stacy."

"This is . . ." she began, but then she couldn't remember what she was going to say. Her brain felt as if it were on fire. Her skin tingled with fever.

Straddling her, Keith rose on his knees, towering over her. He yanked off his shirt, and his tanned chest gleamed in the moonlight above his low-slung jeans. He brought her fingers to his lips and kissed each one, smiling as she gasped with pleasure.

Then he crouched down and dotted her face and neck with kisses. He looked like a lion-man, with his mane of tawny hair, his feral eyes, and she swallowed deep in her throat as pure, white-hot emotion engulfed her.

"Want me, need me, make love to me," he chanted. "Take me, Stacy. I'm yours. I'll do whatever you desire. I only want to please you."

This new song aroused her more potently than the Hawaiian one. Never had a man spoken like this to her, pleading with her to tell him what she wanted. Keith's entire being was focused on pleasing her. The realization both thrilled and awed her. Had she ever had so much power? Had she ever mattered so much?

"What do you want?" he asked urgently, kissing her neck. "Tell me."

She grew shy as the wildness of the moment faded away. Had she really clutched at him? Whimpered like a crazy thing, thrusting herself at him?

"I . . . don't know."

He lowered his head to the creamy flesh above the bodice of the muumuu. That such soft lips could feel so hot!

"No, of course you don't know," he whispered. "You've spent your lifetime in your head, not your body. No one has ever awakened your senses. You may as well be a virgin, Stacy. And I'm honored to be the first."

"But—"

He smiled lovingly. "Hush. Don't protest. From your responses, I know I'm right. No one has fully made love to you. No one has been man enough to subdue his pleasure for yours and show you what you're capable of."

"I—I don't understand."

He laid his head on her breast and held her, rocking slowly. "Your mind doesn't. But your body will."

And then he cupped his hands over her breasts, as he had back in the motel. Unimaginable sensations shuddered through Stacy as he filled his palms with her. She whimpered and averted her face, embarrassed.

"No, love, my little love," he said. "There's no shame here. There's no reason to hide your reactions from me. Your desire is my triumph, *ipo*. Your joy is my joy. Believe that in this moment I exist solely for you."

"What about . . . you?" she asked, gasping as he

fondled her, stroking the ripening buds of her nipples with his nails. Rings of excitement fanned outward, as if Keith had plunged his fingers into the pond of her being and caused ripples on the once-smooth surface. And beneath the surface, more feeling churned in an undertow that soon would sweep her completely away.

"Don't worry about me. Don't think of me at all."

But he was all she could think of. All other thoughts drowned in the expanding sea of pleasure. Only Keith's face bobbed before her, his eyes twin blue lights, the moon a halo around his hair. His body gleamed with unnatural light, as if his heart glowed within his broad, muscled chest.

She kept expecting the seemingly endless attention he was paying to her to end. At any moment she thought he would hurry her along, impatient to make love. But as he caressed and fondled her without even undressing her, she began to realize that he had told the truth: There really was no sense of time in paradise.

"We have forever, little *malihini*," he murmured, as if reading her thoughts. "We have until the end of forever to make love tonight."

"I keep trying to hurry," she confessed. "Thoughts start to pour into my head."

"Habit," he said. "You must learn to concentrate on your feelings as much as you do on your intellect. You must learn to feel desire."

She smiled shyly. "Oh, I feel that."

"No. You've only had a small taste. You're still a virgin, Stacy."

He cradled her breast in his hand. "Do you like that?"

Closing her eyes, she nodded.

"Don't be embarrassed. Look at me." He paused. "Stacy, look at me."

When she opened her eyes, he lowered his head to her breast and kissed it through her clothes. His warm breath made her stomach contract and her thighs tense. She clasped his head and held it against her body, and he reached up and covered her hands with his.

Carefully he closed his teeth around the taut point and sucked. She inhaled raggedly and held his head more tightly.

"Ah," he whispered. "You like that too."

"Yes."

"And this." He kissed her other breast in the same way.

"Yes."

"And this." He moved lower, kissing her stomach, and then lower.

"Oh!" she cried. "Yes!"

He lingered there a moment, then rose on his knees. Stacy gave a sigh of disappointment as he broke contact with her body.

He chuckled. "Now you're giving me the messages I want," he said. "I'm beginning to know what you like."

She swallowed. "But don't all women want . . . the same things?"

"I'm not interested in all women at the moment," he replied, kneading her taut thighs. "I'm only interested in you."

The more he massaged her legs, the tenser they became. "Relax," he ordered her. "Put yourself in my hands. Melt into my movements."

"You must be getting impatient with me," she said softly, tugging at his wrist. "Please, I'm becoming more nervous wondering if you're enjoying this. Maybe we should just, you know, do it."

He shook his head. "A moment ago you forgot yourself and opened to me like a flower. I could feel your desire. There's a lot of passion inside you, and I want to experience it. I want you to know what it is to simply revel in ecstasy. We have forever," he reminded her. "Let's take forever."

He continued to massage her thighs, sliding between her legs over the folds of the muumuu without touching the delicate triangle that warmed and quickened and yearned for him. Not touching her there was almost more exciting than if he had. Eager for him to do so, she stirred. He put his hand on her chest and eased her farther into the billows of petals.

"Go limp," he said. "Just feel."

He stroked her knees, then cupped them, working each joint with his thumb and fingertips. Her lids drooped as first unbelievable tension welled inside her, then disappeared. Her body was a Pandora's box of pent-up nervous energy, and Keith's hands were finally freeing her of it. The cycle was repeated as he moved to her calves, then to her ankles, then to her feet.

"Lots of tension here," he said after he took off her sandals and put them on a rock. He made a fist and rolled it along the arch of her foot. "I've never seen anyone so coiled." He worked on her toes. "You should have a massage every week."

"You're hired," she said, blushing.

He grinned his sassy, crooked grin and winked. "You've got yourself a deal. Now I'm going to turn you over."

"My back?" she asked hopefully, rolling onto her stomach.

"These shoulders of yours," he said as he knelt over her and ran his hands over her shoulders and down her spine. "I can imagine the shape you're in by the end of the day, lugging around tons of books and papers. And I bet you've got a briefcase, too."

"Guilty."

"And you're carrying so much else. You should've been born here, Stacy. The love my family bears for each other . . . We have never known poverty, emotionally or financially."

But what about his father? she wondered. His parents' divorce must have caused strain and unhappiness for him.

"You're thinking again," he warned gently. "Stop it."

"Yes, *bwana*."

"I'm your *kahuna*, not your *bwana*. You're on the wrong continent."

"I don't think so," she murmured. Her shoulders sagged into the flowers. She hadn't realized how stiffly she had been holding the muscles, until Keith moved them back and forth and they resisted him. But with long, easy strokes he prodded them into surrendering their long-held rigidity.

Then he did her back. She moaned aloud when he set to work on her neck and the back of her head.

"You'd better watch it," she said. "I'm getting so relaxed, I might fall asleep!" It was incredible to believe that a few minutes before she had been highly aroused.

"I wouldn't mind a bit," he replied. "You'd wake up again. And I'd be here." He kissed her between her shoulder blades. "And I would have the pleasure of holding you in my arms as you sleep."

His words moved her. She felt a sharp pang below her heart. "Oh, Keith," she whispered to herself. "Are you real?"

"Did you say something, *ipo*?"

"No," she said quickly. "Nothing."

His big hands kneaded the small of her back, then moved to her small, round bottom.

"Oh," she said, mortified.

"You'd be surprised how much tension you've stored up here," he said, pressing his thumbs into the flesh.

"Ouch, you're right," she said through clenched teeth, raising her head.

"Ease into the tension, then let go. That's right. That's good. So good."

Never breaking contact, he trailed his hands down to her feet. Then he began to work his way up the backs of her legs.

"Feel good, honey?" he asked.

"Oh, yes." She rippled like a fish. "It's wonder—Oh, Keith, what are you doing?"

As she spoke, he slid his hands beneath her muu-muu and touched her bare skin.

"We've gotten rid of the bad tension," he said softly. "Now let's create some of the good."

"Keith . . ."

"You're ready now. Do you feel it?"

She paused. He was right. She had never felt so refreshed in her life. She was relaxed, but not in a sleepy, groggy way. Her body was cleansed of the need to hurry and worry and defend itself against a threatening world. For the first time in so long, she felt young and strong . . . and desirable.

"Yes, you do feel it," he answered for her. "Oh, boy, do you feel it."

His fingers traveled over the backs of her knees, up her thighs, and lingered at the edges of her panties. The core of her feminine being seized as he spanned his hands over her flesh and his thumbs slid inward toward the soft skin.

Then he pulled his fingers together and swept under her panties and over her bottom. She caught her breath and raised herself up on her elbows, looking at him over her shoulder.

He was no longer smiling. With a swift motion, he looped his thumbs through the waistband and slid the panties over her bottom and down her legs.

As he did so, she turned over. Her muumuu twisted around her hips and wrapped across her upper body, outlining her high, jutting breasts.

"My mermaid," he said. He dropped the panties beside him and clasped her knees as if to part them.

But the muumuu prevented him. Chuckling, he moved to her side and nuzzled her cheek.

"Love, please untie yourself," he asked teasingly. "I promise I'll be gentle."

Before she could respond, he put his arms around her and lifted her up. They clung to each other.

"Oh, you," she said, and offered her lips to him.

"Oh, me." He kissed her.

Long and lingering, a moonlight, forever kiss. An innocent kiss that was thrilling and silken and made Stacy's already loose muscles slacken so that she could barely move. She dangled like a marionette in

his embrace, giving herself up to the joining of their
mouths even as she would give herself to the joining
of their bodies.

And hearts.

And souls.

She raised her arms above her head and he gathered the muumuu up and pulled it off her. She was
clad only in her lacy bra, and he seemed just as
naked in his low-slung jeans. His chest expanded
with his breaths, his abdomen tightening as he saw
her nearly nude body for the first time.

"My Anastasia," he murmured, laying a possessive
hand on her hip.

Hesitantly she covered his hand with hers. "My
Kika."

He kicked off his sandals and put his hand to the
snaps on his fly.

"Now is the moment," he said, and she nodded.

The snaps made a muted ripping sound as they
opened. Stacy could barely hear them above the roaring in her head. Fascinated, she watched as Keith
snaked his pants over his hips, taking his underwear off at the same time. He hesitated a moment as
the denim moved passed his pelvic bones, then peeled
his clothes down to his ankles and off.

He was magnificent in his nakedness. His body
was perfectly proportioned, and the fierce glory of
his flesh, his manhood, rose proud and unashamed
as he stood before her, legs spread wide apart. He
was totally uninhibited. He let her study every inch
of his body, reveling in her appreciation, perfectly
content to stand there until she had her fill of looking at him.

"And now one more thing," he said, indicating her
bra.

She took a step toward him, and he reached behind her to unfasten the hook. His body heat radi-
ated from his chest and arms and he smelled of
plumeria blossoms. She wanted to touch his chest,
but somehow didn't quite dare yet. Now that he was

naked, he seemed like a different man, and some of her shyness returned.

"Hey, it's me," he said, and she wondered if he could honestly read her mind.

With a radiant smile he drew away the wispy bra, easing it over her arms, moaning deep in his throat when at last her breasts were revealed to him.

"Stacy, how lovely," he said, and dropped to his knees. With his arms around her back he buried his face between the pale globes, then kissed each one reverently, filling his mouth with the taut, tingling points.

"Seashell pink," he said, looking up at her. "I should have expected that from a mermaid's bosom, I suppose."

His light remark helped to reassure her. Yes, this was the same Keith, the jokester, the gregarious cousin, the adoring grandson. This was the man who had held her last night and told her of the *menehunes*. This was her lover.

When he tugged gently on her hand, she sank into the flowers. Facing each other, they didn't touch for a span of heartbeats, and then they were in each other's arms, cleaving to each other.

Her breasts flattened against his chest as he crushed her against him. They were pressed together like one person, one flesh, one living, undulating being. His manhood thrust against her tight, flat stomach, and she gasped when she felt its heat.

Their kisses were wild, frenzied, abandoned. Stacy struggled for air, but eagerly returned to Keith's lips before she'd inhaled enough.

He grabbed handfuls of her hair, and she his, and they rolled their heads as they kissed every inch of each other's faces.

"Your hair is like silk," he said, panting, and she nodded with a shining smile.

"So is yours."

"And your body is as smooth as obsidian."

"Yes!"

"And you feel so good in my arms, Stacy—"

"So good, Keith—"

They tumbled into the flowers. Petals flew everywhere as he rose above her, kissing her neck, her collarbones, her breasts. She reached for him and explored his neck, his chest, the tiny nipples buried in curly sun-streaked hair.

"Mmm," he groaned, hunching his shoulders as she caressed and fondled him. "Oh, Stace, I'm on fire."

Her last trace of shyness vanished. Now she was a greedy wanton, touching him everywhere, tracing the ripples of muscles in his abdomen, the long ridges in his back, the rock-hard hillocks of his bottom. She took over, gathering him in her arms, and then she began to kiss the places she had touched, moving lower and lower. . . .

"Careful, careful," Keith warned through his gasps. "I don't want to end this too soon."

"There's no time in Eden," she rejoined, ignoring his mild protests. She did exactly as she wanted with him, pleasuring him, rejoicing with each cry that flew from his lips. "And we can always start over."

"You . . . learn . . . fast."

"It's my trade."

He grasped her shoulders and pulled her up onto his chest. Her hair streamed around her, and he lifted it up and let it fall over his neck and shoulders. His eyes shone.

"Now, my love?"

"Now."

Carefully he rolled over so that she was on her back and he was on top of her.

"My virgin queen," he whispered, easing her legs apart. "*Aloha au ia 'oe*, Stacy Livingston."

Then he joined their flesh together. Stacy cried out, giving voice to her joy, and she thought she was going to faint with the sheer ecstasy of becoming one with him. Pleasure surrounded her, pleasure pulsated inside her. She had never known such rapture. The world was a golden ball spinning around her, and Keith glowed in the center of it like a god, moving above her. His smile lit up the night sky, and the petals beneath his hands and knees sparkled.

"You, you," he chanted. "Stacy, love me."

I do, she answered silently. *Oh, I do, I do, I do!*

He quickened his pace. She answered it. They were creatures of the sun riding an endless aurora of such intensity that they had to hold each other tight, tight. They were buffeted by the exquisitely agonizing power of the strongest force in nature . . . the force of life itself.

And joy. And love.

"Never . . . " Keith began. Then his smile faded. His forehead crinkled with concentration and he bit his lower lip as if in a struggle to prevent himself from ending the journey.

"Please," Stacy managed to say.

"Not yet," he insisted. "Not until you're lost too."

They moved as one. The waterfall rushed over them, shielding them from the world, drowning out their cries, until at last the fever gripped Stacy as it had Keith.

"Oh!" she cried out as she burst into a million rays of light.

She was soaring, floating, spinning. Keith was with her and yet he was not; he was everywhere, everything, every moment that pulsated through her veins with golden energy.

Then, just as she was cresting, he shuddered against her neck, and she knew they were together in their bliss.

Gracefully, like swans' necks, their arms relaxed and held each other. Their lips met and exchanged the most loving, gentlest of kisses. Stacy's head sank into the plumerias and Keith's rested against the wild throbbing in her neck.

Stacy thought she heard Keith's love chant, sung by deep, distant male voices, but she knew she was just imagining it. Yet when she lifted her head to look at him, his lips were moving.

"Did you say something?" she asked.

"No. Just thinking," he murmured. He rolled onto his back and pulled her into the crook of his arm as easily as if she were a little child.

"Let's rest, *ipo*. I'm so exhausted, I can't even raise my head."

"All right."

He snuggled her against him. Stacy allowed him to, but already the warm glow of their lovemaking was beginning to dissipate. In its place she felt raw panic: *What had she done?*

Her heart began to hammer. How had she allowed this to happen? What had she been thinking of?

Keith stirred beside her. "Hey," he whispered. "Hey."

She kept her gaze focused on his muscular chest. "Yes?"

He lifted her chin with his thumb. His smile was radiant, his face rosy. "I'm glad this happened, Stacy. I hope you are too." He kissed her and rubbed her nose with his. His heavy lashes tickled her cheek as he pecked her chin before he lay his head back down.

She shut her eyes tightly. Was she glad? she asked herself. Half of her wanted to climb the mountain above them, fling her arms wide, and embrace the stars. The other half wanted to weep.

She had known what would happen to her if she made love with him. Bad enough before, when he had begun to preoccupy her thoughts, distracting her from her vital work. But now that they had joined together in the tenderest, most sacred way a man and woman could, he had filled her heart. It didn't make any sense—she hardly knew him!—but she knew, now that they had made love, what she felt for him *was* love.

She loved Keith Mactavish, a man who was practically a stranger. A man who was inappropriate for her, who had not a single thing in common with her.

A man whom she would have to leave in less than three weeks. But she loved him nonetheless.

And knew, with an agonizing certainty, that he

didn't love her. He would be appalled, or amused, or both, if he knew that she had fallen head over heels in love with him. In three short days he had captured her heart utterly. And she? Had she affected him at all? By the soft smile on his face and the way he sighed in his sleep, she doubted she meant more to him than a pleasant interlude that he soon would add to his memories of the women who had passed his way but once.

For her the heavens and the earth had moved. They were still moving. As she stared at him while he slept, her heart nearly burst with the newness of her love.

He was beautiful in his slumber, a resting god. Tears filled her eyes.

"I'm such an idiot," she muttered wretchedly, and, through the lonely night hours, kept her vigil at his side.

Seven

While the stars in Lady Hina's dress twinkled and gleamed, Keith dreamed. He dreamed of mermaids and sunken treasure, of bonfires and two eyes of emerald fire. Unexpectedly, he dreamed of his father, playing with Keith himself as a baby. Gerald tickled him under the chin and said, "How I love you, boy," then handed him to a woman dressed all in white. She wore a veil, and as baby Keith lay in her arms, he could see beneath it.

Eyes of verdant forest green gazed lovingly down on him. . . .

Keith awakened with a smile on his lips. Wrapped in his dream, he stretched and reached expectantly for Stacy, then opened his eyes when she wasn't beside him.

"Stacy?" He sat up.

There was no answer, and no Stacy. Puzzled, he rose to his feet and walked through the carpet of plumerias.

"Hon?"

Ah, there she was, sitting beside the river, throwing petals into the moving water. He was sorry to see she'd put the muumuu back on, but the lovely picture she made caused his heart to tighten. So winsome, staring into the water. She looked just like the statue of Hans Christian Andersen's little mermaid in Copenhagen harbor. How had such a woman stumbled into his life?

"Hey," he called, but she didn't hear him. Naked, he sauntered toward her. His body quickened as he remembered their tumultuous lovemaking, and he found himself yearning for more. What a wanton she had proved to be!

And yet there had been a vulnerability about her. . . . Even now a strong protective urge made him slow his steps in case he would be disturbing her. He felt again that odd tugging as he looked at her. She was different from the others, somehow. More . . . what? More beautiful? More desirable? More fascinating?

He loved her.

The thought hit him so hard he grabbed his abdomen. He froze, utterly overwhelmed. He loved her! Oh, yes!

He had cried the words to her in his passion: *Aloha au ia 'oe.* I love you. He had meant them then, but in a different way. He loved all women, as he loved all beautiful and wonderful things: life itself, the vast, blue ocean, the sweet mangoes that grew around Tutu's house. His family. The tourists who came to his restaurant. His Hawaiian soul had told Stacy he loved her in that joyous, all-encompassing way.

But it had lied. Oh, it had lied!

"Oh, Kapono, I'm sorry," he whispered. "You were right. And now I'm in trouble."

A disease. Maile, too, had seen it before he had, when she said he had met his match. And Tutu, with her sly smiles, she had known he was losing his heart.

Losing his heart? Good grief, he felt as though he were losing his mind!

At that moment, Stacy turned her head in his direction and saw him. Quickly she looked away.

Oh, adorable angel, he thought. She was feeling shy again! He smiled lovingly, but as he recalled his predicament, the smile slipped.

He was in love with someone! A mainland woman, to make matters worse!

He looked toward the heavens. "What have I done to deserve this?" he asked plaintively. "Haven't I been good?" He could almost hear the laughter of the gods.

Sighing, he scratched his head. *Now* what?

Stacy glanced at him. Summoning his courage, he fixed an unconcerned smile on his face and walked over to her.

"Hi," he said, sitting beside her on the boulder.

"H'lo." She sounded as tense as he felt.

"Couldn't you sleep, *ipo*?" He touched her arm. She stiffened. Confused, he drew away. Had he somehow insulted her?

"I have to get back," she said without looking at him. "I have a lot to do tomorrow and I'm still jet-lagged."

How thoughtless of him. The poor darling was probably exhausted. He nodded solicitously and climbed off the rock. "Let me throw on my jeans and we'll leave."

She tossed a handful of blossoms into the water. "Thanks."

He watched her for a moment, then went in search of his clothes. He was curiously deflated. Somehow, he'd thought falling in love would be more . . . epic than this. That bells would ring and fireworks would shoot off and a chorus of heavenly voices would fill the sky.

Maybe it wasn't love, he thought hopefully. After all, not even the soppiest romantics fell in love in three days. Three days! This couldn't possibly be love.

But even as he denied it, he knew the truth. He was infected, pure and simple.

He dressed without ceremony and they walked back to the car. During the drive to the motel Stacy was edgy, almost irritable. She didn't respond when he tried to joke with her to hide the tumult of emotions roiling inside him. There were joy and confusion and abject, clammy fear.

Too soon they were back at the motel. He wanted to talk to her, but she seemed standoffish, and when he tried to hold her hand, she walked on ahead.

He frowned. She was not behaving like a woman in love. Had he been the only one to catch the fever?

Obviously, he answered himself, which he could understand. No one fell in love so fast. No one, that is, except for a man who thought he would never fall in love at all.

"Stacy," he said as she unlocked the motel-room door. "We—I—need to—"

She opened the door and practically leaped over the threshold.

"Well, hello!" she said to Olga.

Keith frowned. Olga's presence prevented any further discussion—or anything else. Right now he wanted to hold Stacy, to bury himself in her warmth. The woman he loved! The woman he *loved!* He felt like laughing and crying at the same time.

He pulled himself back to the moment. Olga was horribly upset about something.

"Is the KGB once more!" she cried. "After Kapono is gone, I am hearing footsteps!"

"Oh, Olga," Stacy murmured, embracing her. "What did we all tell you yesterday morning?"

"Yesterday morning, yesterday morning! Long time ago, as far as I am concerning! I tell you, Anastasia, is a man sniffing for me!"

Keith patted Olga's beefy arm. The large woman was shaking with terror. "Would it make you feel better to stay at my grandmother's?"

Olga's eyes shone with hope. "Oh, is too big imposing. We cannot."

"It's no imposition at all. I promise you, Tutu wouldn't mind. Come on. Why don't you two pack some things and I'll take you on over?"

Glancing at him over Olga's shoulder, Stacy actually looked angry. "We can—"

"Everything is already packed," Olga said sheepishly. "I wanted to make Anastasia move elsewhere soon."

"Tomorrow we'll see about another place," Keith said. "I have something in mind closer to the caves." Perhaps Stacy was reacting harshly because she was embarrassed to intrude on Tutu, he thought. But didn't she know Tutu adored her too?

"Good," Olga said. "Everything is ready, inclusive of textbooks and calculator. So we can check it out."

"But . . ." Stacy shifted her weight and ran a hand through her raven hair.

"*Please*, Anastasia."

Stacy's shoulders sagged. "All right, Olga. For you, I'll do it."

"*Mahalo*." Olga walked around her bed and grabbed up two suitcases as if they contained nothing but feathers.

"Here, I'll take those," Keith offered.

"*Mahalo*," Olga said, handing them to him. They were so heavy, they nearly wrenched his arms from his sockets.

"This way, ladies." He opened the door and waited for them to precede him, then staggered out into the hall.

"This is wonderful. Thank you," Stacy said the next morning as she inspected the little cabin on the edge of the water.

Keith's cousins the Chings owned a small cabin situated directly across the water from Emerald Eyes. They were delighted to offer it to the *hui* Mo'okini's guests from the mainland. It was a small, two-bedroom affair with a kitchenette and a bathroom and, best of all in Stacy's eyes, an old teak desk where she could do her work. It was also rather isolated, which suited Olga.

"Let KGB find me here!" she said.

Keith winked at her. "That's telling 'em, Olga." He adjusted the air-conditioner and leaned against the windowsill. "Now, I was thinking about getting Kapono and—"

Olga said, "I am having nothing to do with *that* one" at the same time that Stacy murmured, "I have to work today."

"Oh." Keith eyed the object of his adoration. He had tossed and turned all night, thinking of her, knowing she was sleeping with Olga in the double bed in his old room. He was in love, dammit, for the first time in his life. But she had scarcely looked at him since they'd made love. Could it be she regretted it?

Or worse: found him undesirable?

"Oh," he said again, dismayed. "Well, then, I'll leave you two. If there's anything I can do—"

"We'll be sure to let you know," Stacy finished for him, walking to the front door and opening it.

"Oh." Perplexed, he followed her to the door and paused on the threshold. He thought about kissing her, looked at her, and decided that at the moment it wasn't a good idea. She didn't look like she wanted to be kissed . . . at least by him.

"Good-bye," she mumbled, flushing.

"Aloha."

He went outside and the door shut behind him. He stared at it for a full minute, arms crossed, brows knit. This was decidedly odd, being shown the door. And worse, putting up with it.

"The hell with that," he muttered, and pounded on the door.

"Yes?" Stacy asked breathlessly when she opened it.

Without a word, he pulled her against his chest and kissed her. She melted against him with a little moan, and her fingers clutched his biceps.

This was more like it! Satisfied, he ended the kiss and stepped away. "I'll come by later," he told her.

Her cheeks and forehead were rosy and her lips

red and full from kissing. She opened her mouth to speak, but no words came out.

"Later," he repeated, and left.

He didn't turn around again, but he knew she didn't shut the door until he had climbed into his Jeep and tootled on down the road.

But he didn't go back right away. Not after a talk he had with Kapono, who was waiting for him at Tutu's.

He found Kapono in a hammock, sipping a beer and wearing a sling.

"Stay away from those two, bruddah," Kapono said. "That Russian *wahine* nearly broke my arm!"

Keith was astounded. "What happened?"

Kapono shrugged. "I only tried to kiss her. She told me not to, but I didn't listen." Some of his old sparkle returned. "You know, they don't usually want us to stop, those pretty mainland ladies. So I tried again. Next thing I knew, she threw me over her head!"

Keith burst into laughter as he imagined the scene. Kapono shook his head, rocking the hammock back and forth. "I'd watch it, cousin. You cross Stacy and Olga will beat the tar out of you."

"Olga's on my side," Keith said smugly as he pulled up a rattan chair.

"Don't count on it, Kika. If you mess up . . ." He rubbed his arm. "I should sue her."

Sitting, Keith patted Kapono's good arm. "Cheer up."

"But she mangled me!"

"I'll take you sailing. We'll grab some beer and a couple sandwiches and fishing poles."

"Well, I was going to check on the restaurant. . . ."

Keith feigned a look of horror. "Bruddah! Are you turning into a mainland businessman?"

"Hell, no! I'm a Mo'okini to my dying day."

"Then let's go fishing."

Kapono smiled. "I guess I was wrong about you

and Stacy. I thought you wouldn't let her out of your sight. Everybody in the *hui* thinks you've gone *pupule* over her."

Beneath his tan, Keith paled. "Well, cousin, she's a pretty woman."

"I'm not talking regular *pupule*, cousin. I'm talking serious *pupule*. Tutu says you're in love."

"Tutu doesn't know what she's talking about. People don't fall in love in a matter of days."

"She said she met Grandpa one day and married him the next." Kapono eyed Keith warily. "She says falling in love real fast is a Mo'okini trait."

Keith snorted. "So is getting divorced, I guess."

"Your mom never wanted to. It was your father's doing. So that makes it a Mactavish trait."

Keith's mouth fell open. *Marriage*? He hadn't thought that far. He hadn't thought at all. For heaven's sake, he'd just fallen in love with her!

But to marry Stacy, to have her here with him and all his family. To have babies . . .

He wiped his face. Kapono was right—he was *pupule*! As crazy as they came. He, married? *Married*?

"You sleep last night?" Kapono asked, raising himself on his good elbow. "You look awful."

But what other course was there? Keith wondered. He couldn't just let her fly back to Minnesota, could he? Let her walk out of his life forever? Leave him?

Perspiration broke across his forehead. *Pupule.* He had to get away, do some thinking. That was what was wrong—he wasn't using his head. He was letting his emotions get the best of him.

"Kika?"

Kapono, help me! he wanted to shout. *Talk some sense into me!*

Instead, he managed a weak smile, and said, "Let's go sailing, cousin."

Kapono didn't look very happy. "Got a lot on your mind, eh?"

"Why do you say that?" Keith's brows rose and his eyes widened in forced innocence.

"Because I know you, bruddah." Kapono shook his head. "Or at least, I thought I did."

Two days passed without a visit from Keith. Stacy found she was both relieved and disappointed. He had gotten what he wanted, she assumed, and moved on to choicer territory. Though she knew it was for the best, her heart broke. Ashamed of her tears, she hid them from Olga, taking long showers or walking in the famed Kauai downpours.

Two days, and then he "just dropped by" when she was weeping in the shower. He chatted with Olga while Stacy fumbled with a towel and her blow dryer, taking more time than usual to dress because she was so nervous and excited. Painstakingly she applied eye makeup to hide the ravages of her crying.

He rose like a gentleman when she came into the room, then sat for a while with them, drinking beer with Olga while Stacy nursed a soda. His demeanor was serious, almost somber. He seemed preoccupied, staring at Stacy all the time with unfocused eyes, as though he weren't even listening to what she was saying. Then abruptly he left.

Another two days passed. He invited them to dinner at Tutu's and was so solicitous of Stacy that she grew even more nervous around him. He filled her plate for her, chose a nice spot beneath a palm for her. He asked her about her work both on the island and back home. He asked a lot of questions about Michigan. As the evening wore on, he grew serious again, and the preoccupied look glazed his eyes. When he took her and Olga back to the cabin, he left quickly, without kissing her. He just stared at her.

One more day dragged by. And now he was back again. Why? If he found her company so unenjoyable, why did he keep returning? He never laughed anymore, never joked. Had he somehow realized she was in love with him? Was he trying to let her down easy? Didn't he know that each time he came around, it made it worse, seeing him and knowing he didn't feel the same way she did?

She knew she should banish him completely from her mind and concentrate on her work, but was unable to spend a moment—awake or asleep—without dreaming of him. Over and over in her mind she replayed their glorious night of lovemaking. Her body ached for him, and when he touched her arm so impersonally when he helped her into the Jeep, or brushed her fingers when he handed her a plate, she thought she would forget herself and throw herself into his arms. Exchanging pleasantries, making small talk, she was afraid her voice would betray her and shout, "I love you!" at the top of her lungs.

She was mulling all this over as she and Olga swam inside one of the Emerald Eyes. In unison they emerged from the water, took out their diving respirators, and lifted their masks over their foreheads. Clad in swimsuits and scuba gear, they were exploring for visible clues to the location of the Pele's Fire spawning grounds.

"You are crazy if you do not want him," Olga said, darting a glance in Keith's direction. He, too, had surfaced, but he was some distance away. Without a word of explanation, he had shown up on their porch that morning, gear in hand, as if he'd known they planned to dive. Stacy wondered if he had been watching them. She'd heard noises in the night that had terrified Olga. Oh, but she was letting her friend's paranoia about the KGB get to her. Of course Keith wouldn't spy on her.

Would he? She really didn't know much about him at all.

He had persisted in believing she was looking for the secret treasure, and so was examining odd-shaped mounds or unnatural-looking coral formations that could hide a pile of pirate booty. She found this both infuriating and endearing. He didn't accept her vague explanation for exploring the caves, yet he was willing to help her anyway.

But other than to discuss his going diving with

them, few words had passed between her and him. Yet for once she could tell he was observing her every move, and the knowledge sent a secret little thrill up her back.

"Crazy, crazy," Olga repeated, "if you are not wanting such a one."

"What do I need him for?" Stacy retorted. "I'm too busy to be thinking of a boyfriend."

"*Husband,* Anastasia. Husband. Valentine's Day is near. Only four days."

"Oh, balderdash! Can you imagine me married to him?"

"Why not?"

" 'Why not?' " Stacy imitated Olga's innocent tone. "Humph." She jammed her respirator back in her mouth, adjusted her mask over her nose and eyes, and plunged back beneath the surface.

Schools of tiny parrot-colored fish swarmed and swirled away from her, sensing the agitation in the water—and perhaps even the agitation in her heart.

Why not? she repeated silently. Because he came and went as he pleased, without regard for her feelings? Because he didn't get worked up over things, not even her? Because he didn't care about anything passionately, as she cared about finding the Pele's Fire?

Because *he* didn't want to marry *her*?

Because he didn't have a miserable, bursting headache, the way she did?

Scowling, she swam in a straight line, not even seeing Keith's behind before she rammed into it.

But ram it she did, bashing into his small, hard buttocks with the top of her head. At once he whirled around and caught her around the waist.

She shook her head wildly. She could see his sea-blue eyes glowing in the clear water as he looked at her through his mask. His grip on her tightened, and she felt a powerful surge of excitement deep within her body. A giddy thought raced through her mind—*Good grief, with all this electricity, we'll both be electrocuted in the water*—then she quelled the mad rhythm of her blood.

Still underwater, he took his respirator out of his mouth. They were scant feet beneath the surface, so when he reached for hers, it was not out of fear of drowning that she began to struggle.

It was because if she didn't move away she would betray herself.

With a firm grip on her wrist, he surfaced, bringing her with him.

The water lapped around her breasts as she breathed into her air tank. Still grasping her wrist, he lifted both their masks onto their foreheads and took out her respirator. His fingertips grazed her lips, and she felt them tingle. At last she managed to speak, though she still wasn't thinking. After days, nerve-wracking and confusing days, of polite distance, he was holding her.

"My headache's gone," she said blankly. "I had the worst headache."

"I missed you yesterday."

Then why hadn't he visited her? she wanted to ask. She wondered—though she didn't really want to know—if on the days they weren't together he was with someone else.

"I missed you," he said again.

"Did you . . . come around last night? We heard noises again."

"There are monkeys in the trees."

She gave a nervous laugh. It seemed the words were coming in awkward bursts. "No, honestly? Monkeys?"

"And *menehunes*." He grinned. "Remember the first time the *menehunes* visited you?"

Swallowing, she nodded. "Did Kapono get his arm checked?"

"All better. Just a strain."

"I've *told* her to be careful. She shouldn't arm-wrestle with anybody. She doesn't know her own strength."

"You don't know yours, either, Stacy."

She wasn't sure what he meant. That oddly serious look had come over his face again, and she wanted to beg him to smile.

"Well," she said, not sure what else to say. "Well."

"We should go out tonight. You haven't been seeing much of Kauai lately."

Or him? "I've . . . uh, got a lot of work," she replied, to remind herself more than him of her obligations.

" 'All work and no play . . .' "

"How would *you* know?" she shot back, feeling defensive, and was chastened by the look of hurt that flashed over his features. "I'm sorry. I didn't mean that." Her tone grew soft, until it was almost a whisper. "Really, I didn't."

As he stared at Stacy, Keith remembered his dream about his father. Stacy would prefer a man like Gerald, hardworking and ambitious, a workaholic. Someone who never relaxed. She had tense muscles and Gerald had ulcers. They would make a perfect couple.

And oh, he was feeling grouchy and frustrated. He supposed it was yet another symptom of this terrible disease called love.

Which he still had, despite his attempts in the last week to shake it. He had thought that if he didn't see her, he would forget about her. But if anything, the absences made him think about her, yearn for her, all the more. He never could stay away longer than two days.

Then all the time they were together, he was in an agony of indecision. What to do: Declare himself and risk being sent away for good? Court her subtly? But how did a man stay subtle, when he was wildly in love, when he spent half his time with her wondering what it would be like to be married to her?

What would she do if he proposed? Laugh? Cry? Sic Olga on him?

What if she said yes? Would they end up like his parents, divorced and unhappy?

No, never! That wouldn't happen to them.

"Keith, I'm sorry." She touched his arm.

"It's only true," he said airily, hoping to conceal his thoughts. "We're such opposites, you and I."

He remembered what else he had said the first time he'd told her that—*and opposites attract, don't they?*

Yes, oh, yes, they did.

"So," he went on, swimming lazily toward the boulders where they'd tied up the dinghy, "how's your work going?"

"I've taken water samples and tested them," she said, wincing. Screwing up her face, she added, "The headache's coming back."

"Poor love." He began to rub her shoulders. She was beginning to tan, he noted. She had never burned. He should've realized a sensible woman like her wouldn't impetuously bare her fragile skin to the strong sun.

"And there's a definite spawning zone near the back . . ." Her voice trailed off as Keith looked at her curiously.

"A spawning zone?"

He stepped onto the underground ledge and took off his air tanks, slinging them onto the rocks. Stacy stayed in the water, ignoring his outstretched hand. She slumped.

"Look," she said in a hushed voice, "if I tell you the truth, will you promise not to breathe a word to anyone?"

His smile was crooked and self-mocking. "My discretion is legendary."

"I . . ." She rubbed her temples. "I don't know why I'm telling you this. I guess I'm just tired of having you think I'm a liar."

"Just a money-hungry mainlander." He chuckled at his own joke. When she frowned, a contrite expression replaced his smile, and he held his arms out to her. "Stacy, please. I'm only trying to kid you a little. What's the matter? Don't you feel well?"

"It's just this headache. I . . ."

Tears formed in her eyes. Keith was alarmed. She must really hurt, he realized. He seldom had headaches—in fact, he couldn't recall the last time he'd had one—but his father did. He could remember tiptoeing around their Honolulu apartment, his mother admonishing him to play quietly because "Daddy's got a lot on his mind."

"Oh, baby." Keith slid back into the water and gathered her up against him.

"Let me go." Her voice cracked and she looked away, hunching her shoulders.

"You've got to relax." He placed his thumb over her left temple and rubbed.

"Relax? When Dr. Martin might refuse to accept the results of my research?" she asked shrilly. Paling, she batted at his hand. "Keith, let me go."

"What are you talking about? Come on, sweetheart, you can tell me."

She sighed. Her next words surprised him. "Is there no refusing you anything? For one so easygoing, you certainly are stubborn."

He said nothing, only continued to massage her head and shoulders. She unbent a little, finally lowering her shoulders and exhaling slowly.

"I told you I was an ichthyologist, right? Well, I think there's an undiscovered species of fish that comes here to spawn. In the literature it's called the Pele's Fire."

He waited. She didn't say anything more. "And?"

He wondered if she was growing aroused, as he was. Their bodies were bobbing against each other's, and Keith was responding to her soft warmth with hard fire. It had been an eon since he had made love to her, and not a minute went by that he didn't desire her. And his desire grew as he saw that inside her blue maillot suit, her nipples were becoming hard and taut and her stomach had contracted.

"I've based my thesis on it," she said. "If I don't find it, I don't get my thesis passed. No thesis . . ." She sighed. "No doctorate."

Keith's hands returned to her temples. "Forgive my ignorance, but can't you just confirm the fish is mythical if it doesn't show up? I mean, won't that count?"

"Not if Dr. Martin's on your advisory board." She made a face. "He's using this to keep me from getting my thesis passed. It's the last way he can block me. He's already tried everything else."

Keith frowned. "But why?"

"He's a real throwback. He thinks women should stay barefoot and pregnant."

Keith stroked the back of her head. "That has its appeal," he said before he had a chance to think. Trying to recover, he jokingly added, "And nobody around here wears shoes. Did you know there are more podiatrist conventions in Honolulu than in any other city in the world?"

She rolled her eyes. "Don't you take anything seriously?"

He started to tell her the truth, that he was taking everything seriously these days, but he shut his mouth. A muscle jumped in his cheek and he closed his eyes. A vision of Stacy in a white wedding gown filled his mind, and his eyes flew open.

Her head was cocked and she was watching him, obviously intrigued.

"Dr. Martin," he prompted.

"Yes, Dr. Martin. On top of everything, I'm terrified he'll talk about my research. If other ichthyologists hear of it, they'll swarm over here and take credit. I didn't know what he was like when I confided in him and asked him to be my adviser," she went on. "Now it's too late."

He nodded sympathetically. "And if the fish doesn't show?"

"He's already told me he'll refuse to accept my thesis. He'll block me any way he can." She wrinkled her nose. "He's got this slimy assistant, Norman DuMont. I can't believe he hasn't told him about it. It would be a coup for anybody to find the Pele's Fire."

"Why hasn't he swarmed down here himself?"

Stacy moaned involuntarily as Keith's fingers worked their magic. He smiled. "I suppose he has some honor left. I don't know. But now you can see why I'm so worried."

She looked at him expectantly. After a pause, he shook his head. "No, I can't. Nothing's worth the pain you put yourself through. Nothing."

She straightened her shoulders and jerked her head away from his touch. More tears glistened in her eyes. "Don't you have any sense of ambition at all?" she demanded, clenching her fists. "Haven't you ever really wanted something with all your heart and soul?"

Just you, he thought. Water and cave whirled around him, and for a moment he drowned in the impulse to tell her he loved her. "Well . . ." he began, his heart thundering.

"Kika! Uncle Kika!"

Stacy and Keith turned to see Lani perched in the stern of a yellow rowboat. In front of her, Paulo Mo'okini sat at the oars.

"Aloha," Paulo called. He rowed up to them.

"Guess who's here!" Lani cried.

Softly, urgently, Paulo spoke to Keith in Hawaiian. At his words, Keith grew stony. Then he turned white. His fingers wrapped around Stacy's shoulder as if for support.

"My grandpa's here!" Lani announced. "Uncle Kika's daddy!"

Paulo spoke again in Hawaiian.

"Stacy, come with me," Keith said. She heard worry and anger in his voice, and her heart went out to him.

"What's happened?"

"Just come."

Looking embarrassed, Paulo spoke again. Keith replied in firm, unyielding tones.

"I think I should stay here," Stacy said, sensing that Paulo had asked Keith to go without her.

"Sorry, Stacy." Paulo shifted to give Keith room in the dinghy. "This is *hui* business."

"But she's like family!" Lani said. "She's got a

kitten and everything! And Uncle Kika's in love with her!"

Paulo covered a smile with his hand. "Lani, quiet, now."

"But he *does* love her! Everybody's talking about it! They say he's going to ask her to—"

"Lani Pilialoha," Paulo said warningly. "Enough."

Stacy was stunned by Lani's outburst. Keith loved her? Could it be? Keith was going to . . . what? Ask her to . . .

To . . .

"I've got to go," Keith said brusquely, dropping his arms from around Stacy. "I'll talk to you later."

When? she wanted to demand. When?

To stay here with him?

"I hope everything works out," she said in a half-whisper.

He touched her cheek. "I hope so too." With a distracted look he climbed into the boat.

" 'Bye," she called, but Keith didn't even turn around.

Stacy and Olga continued to explore the caves until the afternoon light grew dim. Then they piled their things into the small boat the Chings had lent them and rowed back to the cabin.

Olga cocked her head and bent low to peer into Stacy's face.

"Hello?" she said gently. "Anybody home?"

Stacy stirred. "I'm sorry, Olgavitch. I was just thinking."

"About Keith." It was not a question. When Stacy didn't reply, Olga let go of one of the oars and patted her hand. "I am worrying for his troubles too. What do you think is big problem?"

"I don't know. Maybe his father's sick. Or his mother. Maybe his father just inherited a million dollars and wants to share it with Keith." She laughed grimly. "He wouldn't like that very much, would he?"

"Maybe Papa is visiting only."

"But they all acted so tense."

"Papa is not popular boy." Olga squeezed Stacy's hand. "Is hard, worrying but not allowed to be with him, *da*? Like you are not part of his life."

Stacy shifted uncomfortably. "I don't want to be, either."

"Oh, really? Then you are moon-eyes for nothing when he is near?"

"Olga, I am not!"

"Mmph. And he, also moon-eyes. You are two pods of peas, I am saying!"

What had he wanted to ask her? she wondered, then she held out her hands. "Let me row. I have too much energy stored up."

"He is providing one good way to get rid of it. Why you are not sleeping more with him?"

Stacy's mouth dropped open. "Olga!"

"I mean it. I knew you are making love when you came back that night with him. You were like little rose and he was looking like he was wanting to kiss your toes! So why so tightup with him? Why not go for?"

Stacy couldn't help but smile sadly at Olga's version of what had happened. And yet she felt that Olga had joined the enemy camp somehow. "What would your Lithuanian grandmother have to say about that?" she asked challengingly.

"Was hot-blooded Gypsy," Olga reminded her.

"Well, then, my scientific assistant, what's happened to rational thinking? What about when our research is over?" She wrestled the oars away from Olga and thrust them forward into the still water. "What happens when the next planeload of sexy birthday hula dancers lands?"

Olga shook her head. "You cannot row from that seat. For him, no more sexy hula girl. I predict."

Stacy handed back the oars. "No way. Once a wolf, always a wolf."

"Lithuanian grandmother, Anastasia."

"Who probably had an arranged marriage. Olga,

we have nothing in common. Nothing. He doesn't even like snow."

"He likes you. That is enough."

"Maybe back in the Old Country."

Olga wagged her finger. "Not to make sniding remarks, Anastasia. I am older, therefore wiser." She cracked her knuckles. "And besides, if he hurt you, I will beat him to a pup."

"Pulp, Olga, and you wouldn't." She leaned forward and kissed her friend's cheek.

Olga's eyes narrowed. "Oh, no? Let him try to hurt you and see."

Stacy crossed her arms defensively. "No, thanks. And that's exactly why I'm not sleeping with him anymore. Besides, he . . . hasn't asked me lately."

"Because you are making like deep freeze to him."

"I am not!" Stacy argued. But she had been, she realized. She scratched her chin. Had he responded in kind?

Then it was all to the better. Think how much worse off she'd be if they had launched into a grand, passionate romance. She was a wreck as it was, with nothing going on between them.

Nothing? This misery was nothing?

Olga sighed. "You wait. Valentine's Day. I predict."

Eight

Later that night, Stacy looked down at page three hundred sixty-five of *Photosynthetical Mitosis in Tropical Invertebrates* and realized she'd read it at least twice already. Or looked at the words, rather. Her mind was nowhere near her work.

Olga was outside, stringing aluminum cans between the palm trees. They clanked and rattled, and Stacy thought of icy mornings back home, being awakened by the noise of the garbage truck after she'd studied most of the night. Shivering, she would wrap her bedspread around herself and stagger into the kitchen to boil water for instant coffee . . . and start studying all over again.

Olga had also dug narrow trenches, in front of the doors and windows and covered them with palm branches. The outdoor lights blazed like searchlights; seated inside, Stacy could watch every move Olga made.

"No more KGB!" Olga called through the window. Stacy gave her a thumbs-up and returned to page three hundred sixty-five . . . for the fourth time.

What was happening at the *hui* Mo'okini?

An hour later—having progressed to page three

hundred sixty-six—she jumped when Olga strode into the room, wiping her hands. "You are still up?" she asked in surprise. "Look how late! We must both sleep!"

Stacy glanced at the clock. It was nearly midnight, and no appreciable amount of reading had been done. With a sigh she shut the book.

"How time flies when you're having fun."

"Not so glummy, Anastasia. I'm sure everything is A-okay with Comrade Sweetie-Pie. I predict."

Stacy nodded wearily. She turned down the air conditioning and slipped into a sleeveless, cotton, eyelet nightie that grazed her knees, washed her face and brushed her teeth, and joined Olga in the double bed.

"I predict," Olga repeated, and fell asleep within minutes.

Soon her snoring shook the house. Wincing beside her, Stacy sat up—and froze when she heard the clatter of cans outside.

"Olga," she whispered, but the large Russian was dead to the world.

The cans banged and rattled.

"It could be monkeys," Stacy whispered as she drew on her matching eyelet bathrobe and minced to the front door.

Carefully she opened it. "Is anyone there?" she demanded. Olga snorted in her sleep.

"Help," came the distant reply. There was more clattering.

"Who is it?"

"Stacy, it's just me!"

She ran toward the trees. "Keith? Keith, where are you?"

"Here! Oh, no! Oh, dammit!"

There was a tremendous clanging and then a crash. Stacy flew deeper into the palms—and almost ran right over Keith, who lay sprawled on his face. A string of cans was looped around his ankles.

"Are you hurt?" She fell to her knees beside him.

He rolled on his side and wiped dirt off his nose. "No. Just surprised. Is this Olga's handiwork?"

"Yes, and she did a pretty good job. You're really tangled up." She searched for the end of the string among the cans. Keith was wearing shorts, and her fingers brushed the blond hairs on his sinewy calves and ankles. His thongs had slipped off when he'd fallen, and she noted a large scar across the big toe on his left foot.

"How'd you get this?" she asked, startled, as she drew the string away.

"Shark bite."

She shivered. A loud snore blatted from the house, and they both chuckled.

"Some alarm system," Keith said. Then his smile slipped. "Stacy . . ."

She looked at him and knew that something was terribly wrong. "What's happened? What's the matter with your father?"

He sagged. "That's a question I ask myself a hundred times every time I see him. Stacy, things are bad for him. . . ." He fell silent.

"How bad?"

Keith didn't answer. His silence unnerved her. "Let's get you untied," she blurted out. "Wow, this is a mess."

He clenched his teeth and turned his head.

"He's so *stupid*," he muttered. He balled his fists and exhaled slowly in a sad moan. "Never satisfied. He's always pushing . . ." He stopped speaking again. "I came to you because—because there was no one else I could talk to."

The silence lengthened. Birds chirped above them in glowing boughs of moonlight, and a strong gust of wind shook the cans still strung in the trees. Keith kept his head turned, and the muted light etched the angles of his temple, cheek, and jaw. He was beautiful.

She touched his shoulder, surprised to feel it moving. He was shaking.

"Keith?"

"Don't look at me," he said in a strangled voice.

"Keith."

He raised his chin. "Stacy, I . . ."

She grasped his jaw and forced him to face her. Twin silver tears streamed down his face.

"Oh." She gasped.

"I know, I know, it's *kapu* to cry in paradise," he said, smiling bravely, but when she put her arms around him he began to sob.

"I'm sorry," he whispered. "I'm so sorry."

"Don't be dumb," she murmured, holding him. She stroked his hair, his back, kissed his forehead. She was filled with the need to comfort him. Where was that sunlit smile that made the heavens glow? His mouth was contorted with pain, his glowing eyes shielded by lids that were tightly shut.

"Oh, poor love, poor love," she soothed in her own chant, wanting so to help him. "What's happened? What's wrong? Is there anything I can do? Anything . . ."

Her words faded away on the flower-scented breeze as Keith buried his head between her breasts. She gasped and held him close, her fingers combing his gold-and-silver hair, so soft that when she closed her eyes she couldn't tell if she was touching it.

"Anything . . ."

His face was hot against her body, his lips seeking the tender, sensitive nipples through the sheer eyelet like a child suckling. And then he became like a lover as his lips grew more insistent.

"I need you," he said hoarsely. "Stacy, I need you."

But he would break her heart, she warned herself before she said, "Yes, Keith. I'm here."

At her words his hands flew over her, touching, branding, as if he couldn't convince himself that she was really there. His trembling fingers shaped her face, her neck, her shoulders. He explored her, claimed her, with those hands that were so powerful and seeking, and yet tentative and careful. His eyes closed, he caressed the length of her back, then brought masses of her night-sky hair across his face.

"It's you. It's really you," he whispered. "Stacy, I've never *needed* a woman before. I never turned to anyone. When Dad left, I was the strong one. Mom was so torn up, I never cried. I didn't want to hurt her too. Everyone said I had to take care of her. But now . . ."

His words both thrilled and frightened her. Though inwardly she rejoiced that she was the one he needed, she was shaken by the change in him. The once happy-go-lucky Keith Mactavish was weeping in her arms like a heartbroken child. She sensed he was crying now for the child who hadn't cried then, for the boy who had tried to be a man for his mother's sake. And for the man now, who was struggling to conceal his weakness from her.

"Keith, I'm glad I'm here."

"I am too."

"Take me, Keith," she said in a rush. "I want to make love."

She helped him slide her bathrobe off and sat still as he took in her body. Some of his old fire returned as his gaze raked over her, lingering on the damp spots on the nightgown caused by his mouth.

Then he cupped her hips and pulled her toward him as he rose to his knees.

"Why did you turn so cold to me?" he asked her. She didn't reply. "Why?"

Still she hesitated. Then she laid a hand on his arm. "I'm warm, now, Keith. I'm here for you now."

He looked down at her with an expression of hurt that made tears spring to her own eyes. "But there's more. Something I must tell you first . . ."

"No. It can wait."

"Stacy, listen to me."

She laid her forefinger across his lips. He frowned and she kissed away the wrinkles. "Ssh. Now is not for talking. Now is for you."

And in that moment, Stacy realized she was about to fulfill herself as a woman. She would offer herself to her lover completely, without hesitation, seeking to give him pleasure he had never known before. For she realized something she had never thought of: Just as Keith had never loved a woman with a special, particular love, perhaps no one had loved him in that way either. He had thought of her as a virgin. To her, he was the same.

She was the first woman who would bring total love to their union.

But after? her mind protested. What about afterward? Would he know what she had given to him? Would he understand the sacrifice she was making, to open her heart to him, to leave herself vulnerable to him?

It didn't matter. That was part of love, making it not matter.

And she loved him. She did! How could she withhold that love from him?

"Stacy, let me tell you first," Keith said, drawing her back from her thoughts.

"Hush."

She molded her hands on either side of his face and kissed him long and hard.

He had satin lips that invited another kiss, and another. His tongue was hot and sweet, and his body quickened when she explored the secret recesses of his mouth. But she held his head, forcing him to submit to her own sweet surrender. Together they sank into oblivion, touching, feeling, loving.

"Hush," she murmured again as he parted his lips. When he reached for her, she forced his arms down to his sides. This was her moment to conquer him, to force him to accept the truth of her love. To be adored and cherished and placed above herself as she gave and gave to him. To move him, to make him the most important living being on the face of the earth.

"No one," she whispered.

No one would ever love him the way she loved him.

She urged him to lie back on the moist, fragrant earth. With shining eyes, he obeyed her. She knelt beside him, asserting her dominion as she surveyed him. Then she eased his shirt up under his arms and traced the whorls of chest hair with her tongue.

"Oh." He gasped, clutching her head. He touched one of her breasts. "Let me undress you."

She pulled away. "No. Tonight it's your turn. Everything I do is for your pleasure."

He reached for her again. "But it pleases me to please *you*."

She pushed his hand away. "Then accept what I have to give you, Keith."

She bent over him and kissed him. He arched up off the ground, and she slid her hands around to the small of his back. His moist skin smelled of coconuts and was as warm as his sunniest smile. Swaying on her knees, she brushed his bare chest with her breasts, exulting in the way his body tightened in response. She felt like a Hawaiian goddess, commanding the restrained force of nature with the merest touch, the softest caress. For the first time in her life, Stacy understood the power she possessed as a woman.

"I will make such love to you," she said huskily.

"Your eyes are glowing," he murmured, undulating beneath her suddenly knowing fingers. "You *are* the spirit of Emerald Eyes." He caught his breath as she pressed against the fullness between his legs. "Oh, Stacy, make love to me, *ipo. Aloha au ia 'oe.*"

"Sing the chant, Kika," she whispered. "Enchant us both."

"You've already sung it," he said, passion slurring his words. "Your fingers are singing it. Your lips."

She rested her head on his chest. "My heart, Keith. My heart is singing it too."

He raised his head to look at her. "Can it be that you love me?" There was a note of longing in his voice that made her soar to the stars.

"Can it be?" she echoed.

They looked at each other in the shimmering moonlight. Gazes locked, Stacy pulled off her nightgown and sat beside him, proud in her nakedness.

"Oh, my darling," Keith said. He clung to her, lavishing kisses on her breasts, her stomach, the dark delta between her thighs.

"Open to me," he whispered. "Open to my kisses."

"Tonight is . . . for . . . you," she managed to gasp out, falling backward into his waiting arms as he rose above her.

"Yes, it is."

He carried her in his arms, deeper into the tangle of trees. The sky broke open and warm rain cascaded down, drenching them.

Within seconds they were soaked. Neither seemed to notice. Stacy blinked against the raindrops as she stared up at Keith, his hair slicked back from his forehead, his eyes burning so that steam seemed to rise from the places he focused on.

There was no shelter. The rain filtered through the branches of the trees and poured down on them. Keith lay her on a bed of red and yellow blossoms and stripped off his shorts and underwear.

He lay on top of her, but Stacy shook her head and wriggled from beneath him. Then she pushed him onto his back and straddled him.

"Enjoy me," she commanded, and joined her flesh with his.

"Woman, woman, what are you doing?" he cried out, clinging to her waist as his body writhed beneath her.

"I'm taking you." She held tightly to his shoulders, reveling in his loss of control. His lips pulled back from his teeth in a grimace of pleasure, and his eyes shut tightly. She threw her head back and the rain streamed onto her face. "I'm taking you as you should be taken . . . with love."

They moved like the rain, falling in a torrent. They were the lightning, flashing and striking, illuminating the universe with their brilliance.

And when the storm quieted, they did too. After the cries of passion and ecstasy subsided, they collapsed into each other's arms. Drained, Stacy was so moved, she cried, her tears mingling with the clean, fresh raindrops that slid off the tree branches onto her cheeks.

With a hand made awkward by exhaustion Keith played with her hair. He squeezed the water from it and curled it around his fingers. The air was balmy and his body was hot. She wasn't in the least bit cold, but still she snuggled against him as closely as if they lay in a field of snow.

"*Auwe*," he said after a while. "It's never been like that for me."

She smiled shyly. "Me neither. I sort of forgot myself."

"No, I think you found yourself. And you found me too. A little part that's lain hidden all these years under the jokes, and with all the women . . ."

He rocked her. "I know I'm intruding on your life, Stacy. You haven't wanted the distraction I pose. And I stayed away for my own sake. I was afraid of the part of me you exposed. After my parents split up, I decided never to make one person special to me." He laughed ironically. "I thought there was safety in numbers. But today, when my father came to me for help, there was no safety . . . except with the one person who *was* special to me."

He looked at her for a full minute before speaking. "That person is you, Stacy. I love you."

She closed her eyes against the overwhelming tide of emotion his words elicited. "I love you too, Keith."

He said nothing more. She opened her eyes.

He was crying again.

They slept then, naked in the forest. The moon dipped into Golden Bay and painted the world with streaks of sunrise. Birds greeted the dawn; Olga's battery of cans clinked pleasantly.

Keith was the first to awaken. He felt Stacy beside him before he saw her, and after reveling in the fireworks glow of last night's memories, he remembered with a pang what he must tell her.

She would be devastated.

"Hon, wake up," he murmured gently. "We have to talk."

Her lids fluttered. Oh, lovely girl, with her blushing cheeks! he thought. She smiled at him and stretched, intertwining her fingers around his arm. "We slept out here all night. What if someone comes along and sees us?"

"The cans will warn us." He touched her cheek. "Stacy, I have something very important to tell you."

His tone finally communicated to her. Tilting her head, she drew back. He caught up both her hands in one of his and helped her to a sitting position.

"Please don't be too upset."

"What? What, Keith? Is it your father?"

He didn't want to do this. Dammit, it wasn't fair.

"You can't use the caves anymore," he said flatly. "I'm sorry, but something's come up."

He had never seen anyone look so stunned. He felt as if he had slapped her or punched her in the stomach.

"I don't think I heard you right," she replied, forcing a smile. "I thought you said I couldn't—"

"I'm so sorry, baby." He moved to hold her.

She jumped to her feet. "You're *sorry*? You came here last night, crying and—and I comforted you and held you and now you tell me you're ruining my life? And you're *sorry*?"

"Stacy . . ." He stood. His body fought his every move. He was so tired and sad, and she looked as if she were going to faint.

"Why?"

He shook his head. Unfair and unkind. "I can't tell you. I was . . . asked not to."

"But you said you loved—" She made a fist and pushed it against her mouth. There were leaves in her damp hair, and where once there had been a goddess, stood a bedraggled waif whom he longed to comfort.

"I do. I do love you."

"I trusted you. I told you about the Pele's Fire, and now, all of a sudden . . ."

He drew himself up. "Are you implying this has something to do with that?"

She raised her chin. Had they the power, those eyes, which had wept for him, would have struck him down. "Why not? Maybe your family wants to make the discovery itself!"

"How dare you!"

Why was he shouting at her? he wondered. Because she had attacked his most vulnerable spot, his love for his family.

"How dare *I*? You knew you had to tell me this, and you let me make love to you first. You kept this from me all that time. You *used* me."

"No, sweet." He held out his arms imploringly. "Don't you remember? I tried to tell you. But I was upset, and you insisted—"

"Oh. I see. It's my fault." Her voice was icy, her look glacial. Her back was stiff as iron. "I beg your pardon."

"Stacy, I know you're upset, and you have every right to be. But please try to understand. They're not just my caves. They belong to the family, and I'm just one vote."

She scrutinized him. "And did you vote for me? Did you tell them to let me keep exploring?"

He couldn't lie to her. Not telling her last night had been a lie of sorts, and he couldn't stand to do it again. He lowered his head and shook it.

"No," he said brokenly.

"So." She marched away from him. "Good-bye, Keith. Or should I say 'aloha,' as you're so fond of doing? Eh, Mr. Fun and Games? Now that you've gotten what you wanted from 'Wondergrind' Livingston?"

"Dammit, that's not what it's like between us, and you know it!" He ran after her and grabbed her arms. He whirled her around so hard, she almost fell over. "You know it!"

"Let go of me!" she shouted.

"No!"

"*Da*!" boomed a command from the porch. Olga

stood there in her bathrobe, with a coconut poised by her ear. "You are letting go of my Anastasia or I am splitting head with kookoonotchka!"

"Olga, for Pete's sake," Keith said, reaching out a hand. "I wasn't hurting her. I love her. I—"

"Away. Talk later," Olga said, hefting the coconut. "Come, Anastasia."

With a sob Stacy picked up her nightclothes and, holding them against her body, ran into the cabin and slammed the door.

Olga stayed on the porch. "Talk later," she said more calmly, then dropped the coconut. She walked down the stairs and toward him. "You are frighten me, Keith. I was thinking you are KGB. Is cause for kookoonotchka." She gestured toward the cabin. "What are you doing to Anastasia?" She made a clumsy gesture toward his lower body. "Besides obvious thing, I mean."

He ran a hand through his hair. He wasn't embarrassed about being naked in front of her. To him, nudity was a natural thing. Still, he covered himself with a palm frond, feeling a little silly, but more concerned about what had just happened with Stacy.

"I can't let you use the caves any longer," he said tiredly. "And I can't tell you why."

Olga made a face. "For Anastasia, is like end of Western world."

"I know."

"You know she love you. Very tightup girl. Thinks your are bad news."

He winced. "I know that too." But loving him in return? No, he hadn't really believed it could be possible until last night. Had he just lost her in the same instant he had found her?

"*Are* you bad news, beach-bum boy?"

He felt like tearing a palm tree out by its roots and hurtling it at the sun. "No! I'm good for her. Olga, I love her like no one else ever could. I would cherish her. I'd take care of her."

Olga crossed her arms. "Then you show her. But go

home now. If you stay, she is beating you to pup with pocket calculator."

Wearily he nodded. "I'll come back later."

"So you say always, thus giving her willies. When? Two days? Three?"

"This afternoon. Tell her."

Olga looked toward the dawn. "Without boyfriend, life is more easy. But you know, is Valentine's very soon." She looked at him as if he would understand what she was saying, then went into the house.

It began to rain. Keith picked up his shorts and snaked them on. "No one ever told me love was a *fatal* disease," he muttered. But deep in his heart, he must have known that. Why else had he resisted falling in love for so long? It was painful and miserable. He was a fool to trust, to care. . . .

Brother, was there trouble in paradise!

Keith glanced at the clock on Tutu Ewa's living-room wall. It had taken longer than he'd anticipated to gather the family for another *hui* meeting. But everyone was here at last, including his father, Gerald, who looked like a man whose life was in danger.

Which it was.

"I've called this meeting because I'm going to go against the wishes of the family," Keith announced without ceremony. "I'm going to tell Stacy exactly why she can't explore the caves anymore."

"But this is family business, grandson," Tutu Ewa said sharply.

Keith squared his shoulders as he faced his grandmother. "Tutu, all my life I've held you in respect. I've obeyed your wishes. But this time I have to go against you."

There was a hushed murmur in the room, then a knock on the back door.

Keith's mother, Nele, got up to answer it.

"Oh, hello, Stacy," she said, glancing at her son.

He, in turn, looked at Tutu—a beat too late to see her secret smile.

* * *

Stacy shifted uncomfortably when she saw Keith's relatives crammed into the living room. A few were in the kitchen, leaning over the breakfast bar. And they were all staring at her.

"I'm sorry. I should have called first," she mumbled, turning to go. "I'll just come back later."

Keith made his way through the crowd. He was wearing cut-off jeans and an aloha shirt of pale blue that turned his eyes to cobalt. As he walked toward her his gaze flicked over her, taking in her khaki shorts and shirt. It was the same outfit she'd worn the day she'd met him, and he smiled as if he remembered. But of course he did. He was that kind of man.

He put his arm around her shoulders and pressed his lips against hers. Startled, she responded before she could tell herself not to. A warmth seeped into her cheeks and found its way into Keith's eyes.

"Stacy, I want you to meet my father," he said, gesturing to a pasty-faced man with thinning blond hair. He was dressed in a pair of dark dress slacks and a white shirt and tie, and he looked hot and uncomfortable. He also looked as though he hadn't slept in years.

"I'm Gerald Mactavish," the man said, rising. "I'm very sorry about your predicament, Miss Livingston." He looked at Keith. "I suppose you have to tell her, son. It's only fair."

"It's family business," Tutu said.

Gerald whirled on her. "And what kind of a family is this, that turns a man's son against him and—"

"Dad," Keith said gently. "Not now."

Gerald touched his hand to his forehead. "I'm sorry, Keith. I know I promised not to bring up the past."

"The family's trying to help you, Gerry," Nele said. "You could show a little gratitude." In a softer voice she asked, "Is your ulcer hurting you?"

"It'll stop in a minute. Go ahead son, tell her."

Keith laced his fingers through Stacy's and led her back to the center of the room. "I know this is family business, Tutu," he said. "But I want everyone to know I consider Stacy part of the family." He faced Stacy. "If she wants to be."

She reeled, but he held her hand firmly, as if willing her not to lose her composure. "*Ipo*, I want to tell you what's going on."

"Kika's going to marry her!" Lani whispered in a theatrical voice. "I'll have a new auntie and she can keep her kitten in his tree house!"

"Ssh," Maile remonstrated.

"My father made a bad business investment," Keith began, but his father waved him away.

"I let myself be suckered into something I knew was illegal," he said frankly. "I didn't have the money to do it, but I thought I'd make a quick killing and could pay everything back. So I borrowed some funds from a . . . uh, questionable source. But it backfired, and now I'm up to my neck in debt to some very tough guys."

"With Italian last names," Kapono drawled. Despite his light tone, he looked crushed as he looked at Keith and Stacy standing close together.

"If I don't come up with a lot of money real fast, I'm . . . dead," Gerald said in conclusion.

"We voted to look for the treasure," Keith added. "Stacy, I know your career is important, but I couldn't risk my father's life for it."

She swallowed, feeling so ashamed. She should have trusted him in the first place. She knew she'd wounded him terribly.

"I—I came here to tell you I'm sorry," she said in a tiny voice, aware of the roomful of people listening avidly. "I was unfair to you."

At that moment she looked past Keith's shoulder to see Tutu beaming at her. Their eyes met. Tutu nodded at her.

"So we have kept our business in the family," Tutu said. "I am satisfied."

"We're going to start looking for the treasure tomorrow," Keith said.

"Perhaps I can help?" Stacy asked. "Maybe we can find it before the Pele's Fire come."

Tutu raised her brows. "The Pele's Fire? That's why you're here? But, child, that's just a legend."

Stacy took a deep breath. "I hope you're wrong, Tutu."

The elderly lady looked smug. "I seldom am, Stacy." She indicated Keith, as if to say, *After all, I knew he was in love with you.*

Later, they ate a family feast of cold cuts and potato salad. Keith called the restaurant and asked for several mango pies to be brought over.

They arrived via one of the sexy lifeguard-waiters, who said, "Boss, you better come by sometime tonight. Jason and Cecilio are quitting, and they want to say good-bye."

"Damn." Keith sighed. "Mainland jobs?"

The waiter nodded. "Cecilio's going to San Diego, but Jason's got something going on Oahu."

Keith turned to Stacy. "I lose them every once in a while. They get *ambitious.*" He grinned at her. "There's not exactly a future in waiting tables at Baggies."

"Depends on what kind of future you want," the waiter retorted.

"Spoken like a native," Keith's father said. Keith frowned slightly and patted the waiter on the back.

"Thanks, Eric. I'll be over in a while."

"Okay, boss."

Eric left, and Keith shot his father a look. The elder Mactavish didn't notice it, and Keith sighed and went back to his dinner.

Stacy was in a daze. Had Keith proposed to her? she asked herself. What else could he mean by including her as one of the family? And his father—was his life truly in danger?

"You're not eating." Gerald sat down beside her, edging out Paulo, who scooted to the right to make room for him.

"You aren't either, Dad," Keith said pointedly. "Stacy, do you want a beer?"

She didn't, but she sensed Keith's need to get away from his father. "Yes, please. And could you check on my kitten? I haven't seen him in a couple of days."

"Okay." Keith flashed her his thanks with a secret, if wan, smile, and rose from the *tapa* cloth where their dinner was laid out.

Gerald watched him go. "My son," he said heavily. "He disapproves of me heartily."

Stacy folded her hands in her lap. "I don't mean to sound rude, but don't you disapprove of him too?"

The man looked surprised. "Sure. Wouldn't you? Thirty years old and he lives like a bum! What has he got to show for himself? Graduated *summa cum laude* from the University of Hawaii and he can't even get credit."

A process that could prove fatal, Stacy thought of replying, but she was too intrigued by this new bit of information about Keith.

"He went to college?"

"Surprising, isn't it? I pushed for it. I wanted him to go into business with me. Then he inherited that damn restaurant with his cousin. It ruined him."

"I thought he was a lifeguard."

"In the summers, to pay for school. Wouldn't even let me spring for it. He's a stubborn one, just like his mother. He inherited the restaurant right after he graduated, and that was that. He came back here and fixed it up. So to speak. What a dump. Threw his education away for nothing. Typical of these islanders."

Stacy bit her lip. He sounded like her, except that there was a bitterness in his tone that made it difficult to listen to his words. If Keith had proposed, if he did propose . . . Hadn't he said all along that they had nothing in common? Hadn't she known she would have to go back to Michigan?

But she had never dreamed he would fall in love with her! She still couldn't believe it.

"But you . . . you married an islander," she said tentatively.

Gerald shrugged. "I know, I know. But she was so beautiful." He looked across the yard at Nele, and his eyes grew shaded with a longing that pierced Stacy's heart.

"She still is, too," he went on. "But it never worked from day one. I was dazzled by her. I was sure love would conquer all, even the differences between us. Where are you from?" he asked, changing the subject.

"Michigan. I'm here to do work on my doctoral thesis."

"The work I put a stop to, huh? I'm sorry, Miss Livingston. Maybe if we find the treasure in time—if we find it at all—you can still find your fish."

"I hope so. I've worked so hard."

Gerald nodded with satisfaction. "Hard work. That's what makes the world go around. But try telling that to this crowd." He patted Stacy's arm.

"Miss Livingston, I like you, so I'm going to give you a little friendly advice."

She smiled politely at him. "Yes?"

All trace of humor vanished from his face. "If you value your happiness, don't marry my son."

Nine

Stacy pretended to busy herself with her plate as she absorbed the shock of Gerald's "friendly advice."

"You seem surprised I'd say that," Gerald said. "But of course you must know how ill-suited you two are."

"Keith hasn't asked me to marry him," she said tightly.

"Oh, come on! That's what that little speech in the living room was all about. If he hasn't officially asked you, he's going to." He smiled faintly. "To be honest, I never dreamed he'd think about settling down. You must be quite a lady, Miss Livingston. In fact, I know you're quite a lady."

He sighed. "You'd be wonderful for him—straighten him up, maybe. But you'd be throwing your life away. He's never going to amount to anything, while you've got everything going for you. I know he's a nice boy, but he's a loser."

Stacy flared. "He is not! He's kind and gentle and witty and—"

"And irresponsible and lazy and he doesn't give a damn about anything."

"He gives a damn about *you*, Mr. Mactavish. He

wept for you last night." She glared at him. "And, given the circumstances of your visit here, I'd like to ask which of you is really the loser."

Aghast, she covered her mouth with her hand. "I'm sorry, Mr. Mactavish. I didn't mean to say that."

His smile was Keith's: mischievous and teasing. "Call me Gerald. I guess I went a little too far too. Truce?"

She hesitated. "Truce."

"I guess that says how much you feel for him. Damn shame." He shook his head.

Did it? Stacy cleared her throat. "It doesn't say anything except that I'm protective of my friends."

"And do you think of Keith as just a friend?"

She had to clear her throat again. "I only just met him. I'm here to do research."

"That makes me feel a little better, then. Maybe he's just putting the make on you. But I'm still warning you to stay away from him," Gerald went on. "He's my own flesh and blood, but I know from experience that he'll bring you nothing but grief."

Keith appeared on the threshold of the back door with a tiny ball of fur cradled against his chest. With feigned nonchalance Stacy speared a chunk of pineapple and chewed it. This was too much for her. Too much.

"Hey, honey," Keith said as he kissed the top of her head. He nuzzled the kitten against her cheek. "The baby's fine. But you haven't named it yet."

She took the cat from him and petted it. Blue saucer-eyes blinked at her as the little creature began to purr. "How about Pele?"

He shook his head. "Half the cats and dogs in Hawaii are named Pele. You've got to think of something original."

Her mind was too full of thoughts already. "You name it."

He chuckled. "I was hoping you'd say that. I already did. Dr. Livingston, meet Dr. Livingston."

"But I'm not Dr. Livingston," she said.

"Yet." He crouched beside her and enfolded her

hands in his. "But I'll move heaven ad earth to help you become Dr. Livingston. We'll find that treasure before your fish comes and then I'll help you with your thesis. We'll do such a fantastic job that Martin won't be able to touch it."

"And what are your credentials for this feat?" his father cut in.

Stacy was touched by Keith's seriousness. "But you don't even think the fish is real."

"I do now."

"Why?"

"I have to. So much depends on it." His glowing eyes caught hers. She stopped breathing, hypnotized by their intensity, and held the kitten so tightly, it squeaked.

"I may only have a bachelor's degree, Stacy, but I'm smart. I can learn whatever I need to in order to help you."

"I believe you," she said quietly. And she did. This was a new side of Keith she hadn't seen before. And to think she'd once accused him of not even liking to read. She felt ashamed.

"Let's go to the restaurant." He urged her to her feet. "I have to say good-bye to my guys."

They would be alone. Her heart skipped a beat. He wouldn't really propose, would he? It was just some mad hope of his family's. . . .

Two days until Valentine's . . .

"Let me say good-bye to everybody first," she begged, stalling.

"I already did it for you." He scratched the kitten behind its ears and finished by tickling the back of Stacy's hand. "Come on."

She glanced at Keith's father. He shook his head. "Remember what I told you," he said. "Give it some thought."

Keith looked at her curiously as they walked to the gate. He opened it and waited for her to go through first.

"What was my father talking about?" he asked, helping her into the Jeep.

"Oh, nothing much." She blushed at the lie. Keith studied her, but was silent. Tight-lipped, he started the engine, and the Jeep lurched forward.

They made small talk on the way to the restaurant. Dr. Livingston clung to Stacy and meowed plaintively as the Jeep bounced along the road, giving Stacy something to pay attention to besides the volcano of emotions seething inside her.

"Hey, Stace. Don't manhandle the baby," Keith teased, once more his companionable self.

The baby, she thought. What would it be like to have a child with him, a sunny, golden-haired boy or a brunette like herself? To see Keith holding her child and his, and loving it more than the moon loved the stars. For he would love it, she knew that, knew he would be the most adoring father a child could wish for. . . .

But what kind of example would he set for an impressionable youngster? When she tried to make their little boy do his homework, would Keith tell him, "Forget it. Let's go surfing." Or to a daughter: "You don't need college. It didn't do anything for *me.*"

She roused herself. Why was she going on like this anyway? She was on the verge of beginning her career—or so she hoped. It would take a few years to get solidly established at some university or research center. She couldn't even think of marrying or having children.

But as they bumped down the road, that was practically all she *could* think about.

The restaurant itself was noisy, and crowded with beautiful women and handsome men. Keith shepherded Stacy around to the back, and they went into the kitchen.

"Hey, guys," Keith said, "where are the defectors?"

The two were fetched. Keith thanked them heartily for all their work, dwelling on the great *hukilau*s they'd participated in.

"You won't have such great surf in California,"

Keith said teasingly. Stacy cringed inwardly. Her doubts about his merits as a father—and a husband— came flooding back.

"Don't bet on it, bruddah," Cecilio replied.

They talked and kidded, but Stacy lost the thread of the conversation as her jumbled thoughts filled her ears. Mechanically she stroked the cat and wondered if she was actually, literally going to faint from anxiety. Wasn't she jumping the gun? He probably wasn't even going to ask her.

"Stacy?" Keith's voice gently sounded through the tumult. "I said, lets go to my tree house for a while."

"W-why?" she said thickly.

"Well, for one thing, you've never been there."

"And for another?"

He laid his hand across her forehead. "Do you have a fever? Your face is so red."

"I'm fine."

"You're clammy." He took the kitten from her. Dr. Livingston was sniffing the air madly. Fish in every direction! Despite her panic, Stacy found it in her heart to pity the tyke.

"We're going to the tree house," Keith said. His tone brooked no protest. Taking her hand, he walked out of the kitchen—but not before he broke off a piece of cooked mahimahi and fed it to the kitten.

There were two ladders to the tree house, one made of rope and one of wood, which was by far the easier to climb. They took that one, and soon Stacy was standing in the most delightful place she'd ever been in.

The entire house was one room, far larger than she'd expected, and it was clean and spacious and airy. Hawaiian fabrics woven in natural fibers covered a sofa and a love seat, blending in with the light wood of a low table and a cabinet that held a television and a stereo system. Both of them ran on batteries, Keith told her as he proudly showed her the kitchen. He had a propane refrigerator and stove, and running water that came from a container on the roof.

Everywhere there were bright pillows and paintings to contrast with the subdued upholstery. Most prominent were finger paintings signed by Lani: Keith on a surfboard, Keith in the restaurant, Keith dancing.

She peered at the pictures. "You're doing the hula," she said.

"Sure. Everyone in Hawaii does the hula. Let me show you."

He eased Dr. Livingston out of her hands and set him on the floor. Then he chose a record from a stack beside the stereo and put it on the turntable.

The exotic twang of a steel guitar filled the room. It was followed by a chorus of voices singing in Hawaiian. It sounded like Keith's chant, seductive and hypnotic, and Keith's body began to move to it as if he were part of the music.

"See? With your feet you go step-together-step-touch." He pointed to his bare feet as the ball of his left foot tapped the floor. "Step. Together. Step. Touch. Good."

She copied his movements. Together they did the pattern until Stacy had it. "Now, move your hips."

He swayed seductively. Stacy gaped. She had never seen a man move in such a way. Back home, a man dancing like this would have his masculinity questioned. But as Keith danced, he looked virile, powerful, and supernaturally graceful. In his cut-off jeans and flashy shirt, he was the most elegant man she'd ever seen. He was totally involved in the music—it was like a living thing, flowing in and around him. When he began to sing with the record, Stacy was overcome and stopped cold, listening, watching.

Loving.

"Don't stop. Here." He put his hands low on her hips. "Do it with me."

She was forced to follow, to undulate beneath his guiding fingers, and soon she began to lose herself too.

"This is a chant," she said breathlessly. "Isn't it?"

"The hula is a sacred dance," he replied, smiling knowingly. "It has great power in it . . . for those who know how to use it."

"You're bewitching me, then."

"Your fault. You bewitched me first." His hands tightened on her hips. "*Aloha au ia 'oe,* Stacy."

I love you. She knew that was what he was saying.

His hands caressed her hips, then moved around her body to fan across her bottom and the small of her back. She caught her breath and he smiled.

"Such fire beneath the calm, cool exterior. Maybe you're not the spirit of Emerald Eyes. Maybe you're Pele herself. Will you burn me, little goddess? Will you consume me with your fire?"

"Keith . . ." She was becoming so aroused, she could barely move.

But he kept up the hula, his sinewy body swaying like a palm in the breeze. He sang to her, and though she couldn't comprehend a single word he uttered, she understood them all.

The record ended, but Keith continued, until at last he crushed her against him and slow-danced. The hardness of his manhood prodded against her lower abdomen, and his heart thundered against her chest. She had a wild, fierce vision of Keith pushing her gently onto the sofa and pulling off her shorts and panties. . . .

"You smell so good," he whispered. "You always smell like roses. Even your womanhood smells of roses. Your skin is as soft as petals. And when you lift your face to me, I feel like the sun."

Unconsciously, she looked up at him.

"Yes, like that." He kissed her, his tongue sliding between her parted lips. "Remember our first kiss, *ipo*?"

She nodded. "Yes, I do."

"It was a love chant." His features softened. "You love me, *ipo*. You told me so. Now tell me again."

She could sense the sudden change in the air. It was as if the gods were leaning down from heaven to see if their chants had worked their magic. She knew Keith was talking about a deeper, more committed kind of love . . . the kind a woman bears for one special man. They were moving toward promises she didn't know if she could make, toward dreams she wasn't sure she could dream. . . .

"What—what does *ipo* mean?" she asked.

"Tell me," he softly insisted.

He stopped dancing and led her to the sofa. She sat, making room for him beside her, but instead he went down on one knee before her.

He took her hand and turned it over, kissing her palm. Shivers mingled with the churning inside her, and she trembled.

"Stacy, I don't have much to offer you except myself. You know how I live. You know what I am. But by God, no man has ever loved the way I love. I know there are differences between us, but we'll work them out."

With his other hand he cupped the side of her face. "*Ipo*, sweetheart, marry me."

She hadn't expected to feel differently once the words were uttered. But now there was such joy in her heart that for a moment she thought she'd actually leaped to her feet. Her soul flew into the sky and rounded the moon, kissing the stars on her flight. Keith, in her life forever! Keith beside her, within her, making children with her! Keith, always Keith!

And then she was sitting on the sofa, with Keith kneeling in front of her, his face a misery of waiting.

Take your time, a voice inside her begged. *Don't rush it.*

"Answer me, Stacy," he pleaded. "I'm dying."

She was so confused! Where only seconds ago she had been soaring with happiness, now she felt small and afraid. Tears slid down her cheeks. Seeing them, all the color vanished from Keith's face. She remembered what he had confided in her—that to save himself from being hurt, he had never let anyone become special to him, and understood the risk he himself was taking in proposing.

"We're so different," she murmured.

"We'll make life together richer for that."

"We want different things out of life."

"But we do want each other." He peered at her solemnly. "Don't we? Tell me you do, my dearest love. Say yes."

At once the happiness broke through the pain. How could she imagine life without him? How could she deny herself the glory of his love?

"Yes, oh, yes!" She flung herself into his arms. "Yes, we want each other!"

"My love!" He caught her up and whirled her around the room. "My own dear, wonderful love!"

He carried her through the room, kissing her and spinning her in a circle, laughing.

Then he ran to a window and rolled up the bamboo blind. "Hey!" he yelled. "Hey, down there!"

Eric, the waiter, opened the back door. "Yeah, boss?"

"Free beer for everyone! We're getting married!"

Eric was agog. "*You*? I mean, that's great, boss. I'll tell the others!"

Keith kissed Stacy again. "You don't mind, do you? We'll celebrate here for a while, then tell my family. Then . . ." He squeezed her suggestively.

"Yes," she said, pressing against his broad chest. "Whatever you want."

But they never made it back to Tutu's to tell the family. After a wild party at the restaurant, Keith could bear it no longer. He led Stacy up the ladder and back into the tree house, and made love to her.

Now sounds in the tree house had awakened him. He turned over, searching for Stacy, and saw her standing in the moonlight with a sheet wrapped protectively around her.

"I don't know," she murmured, and Keith opened his mouth to respond.

But he saw that she was holding the kitten, stroking it as it stared up at her with its huge, unblinking eyes.

"I mean, I was so excited when he asked me. So *nervous*. But now I'm not so sure. . . ."

Oh, no. Second thoughts. Keith's blood turned to ice. She had looked radiant when she said yes. Surely the idea that they might marry had occurred to her before he'd asked her. She must have pondered it, the way he had.

His heart beat so fast, he was afraid he would have a heart attack. When she walked toward the bed, he closed his eyes and pretended to sleep.

All right, then, he thought. He hadn't won her yet.

But he would.

It seemed to take forever for Stacy to fall asleep, but after she did, Keith rose and threw on his shorts, not bothering with a shirt, and shimmied down the rope ladder. He grimaced when he started up the Jeep— surely it would wake her—and urged the trusty old heap onto the highway.

In record time, he was at the Chings' cabin. And true to form, Olga's snores were shaking the trees.

This time he avoided her boobytraps and slipped through the front door with an extra key.

"Olga, wake up," he said, jiggling her arm. She was wearing a football jersey that fit her large frame perfectly. "Wake up, please."

"Mmpf? Huh? KGB?" She rattled off some words in Russian.

Keith sat beside her. "Olga, it's me, Keith. Wake up."

She wiped her brow. "Keith, you are making me terrorized! What now?"

"I asked Stacy to marry me."

She gasped, then bit her lip and clasped her hands together. "*Da*? And?"

"She said yes."

"She said yes! She said yes!" Olga bounced in the bed and threw her arms around him. He was engulfed in woman and football jersey, and when she kept squeezing he was afraid he would pass out from lack of air.

"So!" She bussed him soundly. "There *is* a God."

He couldn't help but laugh. "Hold on there, Olgavitch. I think she might change her mind."

"Tragedy!"

"I agree. So you've got to help me. Give me some advice." He held out his arms. "*Do* something."

She cocked her head. "What, I am like fairy grandmother?" She chuckled. "From Lithuania? In time for Valentine's?"

"What?"

She shook her head. "Not to mind, Keith. I am having bizarre Soviet sense of humor. But you are having troubles with Cinderolga, *da*?"

"*Da*."

"Humph. She is not knowing what she wants, such stupid girl. Books and fishes. Is no life for my Anastasia. Babies." She grinned at Keith. "You would be good at producing such nice babies. You possess excellent equipment."

He laughed and shook his head. "You're too much."

"So says your cousin, Kapono. He is sniffing around me once more, like dog." Her cheeks reddened, and though she tried to look severe, her lips turned upward. "He is hassling."

"But cute, eh, Olgavitch?"

"Well, maybe. But so are you, and Anastasia is still doubting wisdom of marriage?"

"Exactly." He sighed. "She doesn't want just another pretty face."

"I see." Beneath the sheets, she crossed her legs. "Okay, *tovarich*. I give you crashing course on pleasing of Anastasia."

He dipped low. "*Mahalo*, Olga, from the bottom of my heart."

She surveyed him. "First thing. Buy shoes."

He frowned. "Shoes?"

"*Da*. Shoes. Is big deal for her, shoes. Believe. I mean."

She regarded him sternly. Keith sighed, sensing

that profound changes in his life were on the horizon. "Shoes it is."

"And a suit."

"*A suit?*"

"*Da*, and you must put pencils in breast pocket, so." She indicated her football jersey. "Like academic professor."

"I'll look like a—what does Lani say?—a nerd," he said mournfully. "A thirty-year-old nerd."

"Exactly. That is what Anastasia finds most pleasing in boys. Old nerd."

He laughed weakly. Olga was off the mark. She had to be. "Maybe this isn't such a good idea after all. Olga, you go back to sleep and I'll deal with this in my own way."

She leaned over the bed and hoisted something up. It was her coconut, and she hefted it in her hand as if it were a feather. She slid a glance toward Keith.

"You, tomorrow, shoes and suit. And nerd pencils. Or . . ." She indicated the coconut. "I know what is good for Anastasia. Husband and babies. You are in position to give these things. So you must."

"You sound like a communist," he said glumly. " 'From each according to his ability to each according to her need.' "

"Never! I am true-blue Western capitalist. I simply have learned about wonderful Western concept of blackmail. For citizenship test." She smiled at him. "Tomorrow, or bam! on your Western head."

He saluted. "Yes, general."

"And that is socialist rhetoric, not communist. You are as ignorant as Anastasia."

"Then we should get along, eh, Olga?"

She pursed her lips. "Don't forget. Simply because you will be married couple doesn't save you in future from me. I am young woman and will live many years. If you *ever* break my Anastasia's heart, it's kookoonotchkas for you."

He smiled fondly at her. "Olga, I love her as much as you do."

"In slightly different way."

"Yes. But I could no more hurt her than cut off my arm."

She looked immensely pleased. "Bravo. That is precise type of boy I am wanting for my Anastasia. Welcome to family, comrade." She shook his hand gravely, then kissed both his cheeks.

"Now, go back to her. If she is having worries, you must turn on charm like faucet." She grinned. "Of that, you are master."

"Yes, general."

"Proper respect. I like." She wiped a tear from her eye. "This is most happy night. I am joyed-over."

"Me, too, Olga. Me too."

He saluted her, then kissed her cheek, rose from the bed, and walked outside.

For a moment he thought he saw a shadow flit among the trees. He walked toward it, paused to watch, but saw nothing. Still, he turned back into the house and told Olga to be careful. He waited a few more minutes, peering out the window, until Olga finally told him to leave.

"I am putting my imagination into your brains," she said sheepishly.

"Now, if only *I* can do the same for Stacy," he said.

When he returned to the tree house, Stacy was still asleep. The kitten was curled up beside her face, purring. Tenderness welled up in Keith as he slipped carefully back into bed.

"Good night, my wife," he whispered. "And you *will* be my wife. You will."

In the morning they dressed and headed over to Tutu's. Keith had called ahead and told Kapono to pick up Olga so everyone could be there for their big announcement.

But by the time he and Stacy arrived, the whole family had figured out what the big news was, alerted by Olga's splendid mood. They crowded around the engaged couple and threw huge leis over their heads.

Soon Stacy could barely look over the strings of miniature orchids, plumerias, and carnations that ringed her neck and shoulders. Lani had threaded matching plumeria headbands for the two of them. Keith's gave him a pagan, alluring air that made Stacy force down her fears and kiss him, which drew wild applause from his relatives.

Then they all headed down to Emerald Eyes to search for the treasure. Out came old family diaries, tattered maps, and scuba gear. Kapono borrowed an underwater metal detector from a friend and they set to work.

They divided into two groups, the dry-land crew and the underwater team. Stacy was one of the dry-landers, while Keith was put on the other team. "We have to separate these two lovebirds," Paulo said, "or they'll do nothing all day but kiss!"

Stacy and Tutu combed the area by the waterfall. Stalactites and stalagmites met in sharp points, attesting to the age of the cave. The entire area looked undisturbed, and Stacy began to lose heart.

For perhaps the twentieth time, Tutu gave her a big hug. "I'm so happy you're becoming one of the family," she said. "Tell me, what are your plans for the wedding?"

The wedding. They hadn't even discussed it—or their plans for their life together. Was she insane?

"Tutu, I'm not so sure there's going to be a wedding," she said honestly, pain in her voice. "It was all so sudden when he asked me. I didn't have time to think."

"You love him." It was not a question.

"Yes, yes, of course I do. But love isn't enough." With tears in her eyes she turned to the stately old lady. "Isn't that true?"

"Kika loved the Beatles when he was a little boy," Tutu replied. "To me, their songs were like the old chants, with their repeated choruses. 'All you need is love.' That's what they sang, over and over again." She smiled. "That's my chant for you and Kika."

"But love *isn't* all you need. Look at Keith's parents."

Tutu sighed sadly. "You know Gerald a little by now. Which would you say he loves more, his family or his money?"

Stacy bowed her head, saying nothing.

"For my grandson there would be no question of which he would choose." She touched her hand. "I know this is frightening for you. I know you two have much to work out. But I know my Kika. He would never have asked you to marry him unless he was prepared to make it work. I think he will surprise you." She glanced toward the water as Keith broke the surface, gestured to Kapono, Olga, and Pat Ching, and then disappeared beneath the water.

Tutu chuckled. "I must confess he's surprising me. I've never seen him work so hard in his life."

"Gerald said he was graduated *summa cum laude* from the university."

Tutu smiled proudly. "That's my boy. He's so brilliant. He's easily the smartest member of the family."

Stacy sighed. "What a waste."

"How, a waste? He has everything he wants. A loving family, something interesting to do with his time, and now, a beautiful fiancée. Would you rather have someone like his father?"

They both looked at Gerald, huffing and puffing among the boulders. He pulled out a handkerchief and wiped his face with it.

"I don't think Gerald and Nele had enough *aloha* in their hearts to make a successful marriage. But you and Kika, now, that's a different story." Tutu looked thoughtful. "Stick with my grandson. I don't think you'll be sorry."

"If I could only *know*."

"No one can know, my new grandaughter. One can only trust. That is the lesson you have taught my grandson. Now you must believe it yourself."

In the next few days, Stacy watched Keith transform himself into a new man—one with drive and purpose. It was he who located all the hunting equipment, even flying to Oahu to obtain those items not available on Kauai. It was he who read books on the subject, then got on the phone to ask advice from trusted friends in the salvage business.

And it was he who generated the cash necessary for the expedition. Every day, after working from dawn to dusk in the caves, he went to the restaurant and cooked. He double-checked Kapono's books. To the astonishment of everybody, he ordered an inventory on supplies, including beer. The restaurant stopped running out of things, and there were no more impromptu fishing expeditions.

But most startling of all, he wore a suit, including a tie—the first Stacy had seen on an islander—and he carried an incredible array of pens and pencils in his breast pocket.

He was a different man, one she didn't know at all. And whenever Olga caught her staring at him in puzzlement, her friend would thrust her chest forward proudly as if to say, See? He is precisely what you wanted!

She wanted to talk to him, but he was so busy now that he didn't have time. Valentine's Day came and went and he didn't say a word, while Kapono gave Olga a huge box of chocolate-covered macadamia nuts. Stacy's fish were due in a week, or so she believed, and he told her repeatedly that he meant to keep his promise to her and find the treasure before that. He began to look as tired as his father, and his golden tan started to fade. Even Tutu looked concerned.

No one knew that Keith was sweating bullets. He hated wearing a suit, and his shoes were giving him blisters, but what was the alternative? When he thought of returning to Michigan with Stacy—and he would, if that was what she wanted—he thought of snow and sleet and more shoes. Boots, even. And what would he do? Open another restaurant? A real one? Become a mainland businessman? Work like this all the time?

He knew Stacy was trying to talk to him about

these very things, and of course they had to talk before they got married. But he had a lot to sort out before he could tell her where he stood. This wasn't the kind of life he wanted at all. So he used the excuse of the treasure hunt to evade her questions, and then put in extra time at Baggies.

"*Auwe*, you're a mess, bruddah," Kapono said one day. "That *wahine* has ruined you. You're more like your old man every day."

"I know," Keith murmured miserably. But he would do whatever it took—*whatever* it took—to make Stacy his.

Time grew so short, they began to search at night. Keith brought in floodlights powered by a generator. He had never seen his family galvanized into action like this—the leisurely Mo'okinis, breaking their backs for someone who despised them! It was hard to fathom—but they were all doing it, including himself. And yet he had another purpose for his labors— to make it possible for Stacy to get her doctorate.

"All this light is going to disturb the Pele's Fire," he said to her one night as he sat beside her on the boulders in the cave. They were munching ham sandwiches provided by Maile and Nele, who were watching the children back at Tutu's.

"We have to talk, Keith," Stacy said suddenly. "I—"

"I know, I know," he cut in. "As soon as we find the treasure. I promise, darling. We will."

His throat was dry as he swallowed his sandwich. When they *did* talk, what would she say? What would he?

Stacy couldn't keep up with Keith's mad pace. He never seemed to sleep anymore—worse, he never seemed to sleep with *her*. He grabbed a few hours— five or six at most—and then he was either diving in the caves or working at the restaurant.

"Is good boy now, *da*?" Olga asked as they piled into Kapono's car and waited for Keith, who was driving them back to the cabin. It was late at night, and Stacy was exhausted. "What you want your husband to be like. Working all the time, just like you."

Stacy squirmed. "I don't work all the time."

"Humph. As you say, balderdash. Ssh, here comes bridegroom."

Keith climbed in beside Stacy and turned on the engine. "Kapono's coming," he said as he kissed Stacy's cheek.

"Humph," Olga replied.

A few minutes later, Kapono slid in beside Olga and said, "Hi, babe."

"I am not your babe," she retorted, but Stacy, peeking in the rearview mirror, saw that Olga was flushed. She grinned to herself. Keith caught her look and grinned back. His eyes twinkled, and for a moment he was the devil-may-care Keith of the early days, with not a worry on his mind. Stacy felt wistful. She missed the old Keith—and she wasn't sure she cared for the new one.

"Olga's going to teach me how to shot-put," Kapono told them as the car wheezed down the highway.

"Am not! You are too lean-brained!"

"Me? *You're* the jock!"

"Anastasia, what means jock? Is not little underwear men wear for protection of male items?"

Stacy burst into a gale of high-pitched laughter. It felt so good after all the tension that she couldn't stop. Soon she had the others joining in.

"What means? Why laughing?" Olga demanded, and that set everyone off again.

Keith laughed so hard, he had to stop driving for a moment. And there he was, the old Keith in all his glory, as he threw back his head and the moonlight gathered in his eyes.

It would be all right, Stacy thought. They would talk and settle things and everything would work out.

Joyously she threw her arms around his neck and kissed him. "Welcome back," she whispered.

He returned her kiss, then smiled at her. "But I didn't go anywhere."

She said nothing, only laid her hand on his thigh as he started up the car and drove on.

She noticed that things had gotten quiet in the back seat, and when she stole a look, she saw that Kapono and Olga, too, were kissing. A smile played on her lips as she turned back around, and Keith winked at her.

Then they reached the cabin. Maybe Olga would go off with Kapono, she thought. Or perhaps Keith would ask her to go to the tree house with him. Or maybe *she* would ask *him!*

She'd come a long way from the bookish woman who had stammered and blushed in front of the exquisite Keith Mactavish, she thought wonderingly.

Musing, she unlocked the door of the cabin. And gave out a cry.

"What the devil!" Keith thundered as he strode past her and whirled around in the center of the room. "What the hell's going on?"

The place was a shambles. Every drawer in the chest and the nightstand was dumped on the floor, and the contents were strewn everywhere. The bed had been stripped and the sheets left in a heap. Worst of all, every one of Stacy's books and papers had been thrown around, with spines broken and pages ripped.

"Did you have any jewelry?" Kapono asked, dropping to his knees.

"Don't touch anything. I'll call the police," Keith said, wrapping a towel around his hand before he picked up the phone.

Stacy balled her hands into fists as she looked at the ruins. "I can't believe this. Who would have done such a thing?"

"A thief," Kapono said with a growl.

Olga burst into tears. "No! Is KGB!"

Forcing herself to remain calm, Stacy surveyed the wreckage without touching it. Her heart stopped. "Oh, no. Keith," she said weakly, "I think my notebook's missing. It has all my data on the Pele's Fire."

He flashed her a look of concern. Then he spoke

into the phone. "Yes, hello. Kika Mactavish. I'm at my cousin Ching's cabin. We need some *kokua*. There's been a break-in." With a tone of authority he gave all the details.

Olga threw her arms around Stacy. "Is KGB! I know!"

Stacy closed her eyes. "I don't think so, Olga. I think I know who it is."

Ten

A policeman arrived at the cabin and took down all the facts, but he wasn't very hopeful about apprehending the thief.

"I hate to tell you this," he said, "but we have a high crime rate during tourist season. It's almost impossible to solve all the burglaries that are committed. I'm sorry."

"Then I'll find him." The ferocity of Keith's tone startled Stacy.

"Now, Kika," said the policeman, who knew him, "don't get riled up. Nobody got hurt. That's the main thing."

"Somebody's *going* to get hurt."

"Kika, calm down," Kapono said.

"So much for no troubles in paradise," Olga grumbled.

"I think I know who did it," Stacy said. Their search of the room had strengthened her suspicions. The only item missing was her precious notebook.

The others looked at her. "I think it was Norman DuMont, or someone else who knows about my . . . theory." She paused, not wanting to divulge the secret of the Pele's Fire to yet another stranger, but concerned that she provide enough information to apprehend the robber.

"Norman's a grad student." Keith filled in easily, rescuing her. "He's jealous of Stacy and could be trying to steal her research."

The policeman shrugged. "Well, we'll check it out. See if we can find any trace of him on the island. And we'll watch the airport, too."

"Thanks," Stacy murmured, heartsick. Professor Martin himself had no doubt told Norman, dishonorable man. Well, it might not matter too much anyway that others knew of her theory, seeing as they hadn't found the treasure yet. No one was going to be looking for the Pele's Fire anytime soon.

After the policeman left, Keith kissed Stacy quickly and said, "I'll see you later, *ipo*. Kapono, set a guard on the caves. If it is DuMont, he may try to sneak into Emerald Eyes."

"But where are you going?" Stacy asked.

"To look for that bastard."

"It's a big island, bruddah," Kapono said.

"Keith, let's you and I watch the caves," Stacy suggested. "I'd feel better." *And I want to be with you,* she silently added.

He hesitated. "Please, Keith. I . . . see you so seldom these days," she went on, embarrassed to speak like this in front of the others.

Though his blue eyes flashed like steel, his expression softened when he looked at her. Yet his jaw was set and there was grim determination behind his look of love. For the first time Stacy felt anger in him, deep, unrelenting fury that he was straining to check. There was strength in him she had never dreamed of. Had he been keeping his emotions in check behind a sunny facade, developed over the years since his parents' breakup?

"Is that what you want, my love?" he asked gently. "For me to stay with you?"

She laid her head on his chest, loving the protective breadth of it, the sure, steady rhythm of his heart. There was more to him than she had guessed. "That's what I want."

"And I'll stay with Olga," Kapono said, throwing his arm around her shoulders. Olga turned red and looked away.

"*Mahalo*, Kaponovitch," she said.

"We'll take the dinghy." Keith gave Stacy's hand a reassuring squeeze. "Don't worry, honey. We're the ones who have possession of the caves. We'll catch these guys, find the treasure, and then the fish will come and your reputation will be made. They won't be able to touch you."

She tried to smile and failed. "I just can't believe he'd steal from me. Now he can claim all my research was his."

"*Nyet*," Olga cut in. "Anastasia, I am back in Michigan every day copying all pages."

Stacy raised her brows. "You mean, you photocopied my notebook? Why didn't you tell me?"

"Express orders not to take notebook out of house." Olga replied. "I disobey. I have many suspicions of other ichthyologists." She shrugged. "I am former Soviet citizen, very paranormal on such matters."

"I think you want the word 'paranoid,' " Stacy said, laughing as she hugged Olga. "Thank you so much for not listening to me!"

She turned to Keith, to find the oddest expression on his face. He looked dumbstruck. When she waved a hand in front of his eyes, he didn't even see it.

"Keith?" she asked.

He roused himself. "Huh?" He smiled at Stacy. "Sorry, *ipo*. Something just occurred to me."

"About the robbery?"

"Is burglary," Olga corrected her. "I have learned in study for citizenship test."

"No, it didn't have anything to do with that." Keith put his arm around her waist. "It was about something far more important."

"What could be more important than that?" Kapono asked.

Olga socked him playfully. He yowled and grabbed his strained arm.

"Kaponovitch, sometimes you are too lean-brained," she said lovingly.

He feigned a look of displeasure. "I guess sometimes I am. Falling in love with a Commie!"

Olga caught her breath. "I am no Commie," she said softly, her eyes liquid with adoration. "I am fine capitalist."

"I think it's time for us to make a hasty exit," Keith whispered to Stacy. She nodded. "Do you need anything to take with you?" he added.

She brushed his cheek with her lips. "Just you," she murmured, swimming in his sea-blue gaze.

They rowed to the caves and turned on a few of the lights. Stacy listened to the roar of the generator and sighed. It seemed to be their fate never to talk to each other, even when they were alone at last. There was no way she could make herself heard over the cacophony that echoed off the lava walls.

"It's warm tonight," she ventured. Keith cupped his ear and leaned toward her.

"Pardon?"

"I said . . ." she yelled, but shook her head. Suddenly she felt like crying. Would they never be able to discuss their situation? On top of everything, a theft of her work! And now this noise. All the pressures she'd been under came crashing down on her shoulders, and her stomach knotted with tension. Her research, the interruption, Keith's proposal—it was all too much. She simply gave up.

"Honey?" Keith put a concerned arm around her. "Are you all right?"

She couldn't even make herself nod. She stared at her feet, willing herself to lean against him, to draw on some of that strength in him that she had recently discovered. But she felt terribly alone and defenseless, besides being confused and frightened.

All she wanted to do was turn back the clock and start over.

He sensed her feelings at once. "My love," he said. His chest vibrated from his words. "My poor love."

He held her for a moment, and the bad clouds parted a little. Then he turned off the generator, plunging the two of them into darkness, and led her toward the little waterfall.

"Walk where I walk," he told her. "I have the path memorized."

She obeyed, staying at his side as they meandered through the shadows. His steps were sure and confident, and she could tell he was shortening his strides for her comfort. Oh, how could she doubt her love for him? With her forefinger she caressed the back of his hand, tracing the veins, thanking God for the perfection of his body and the depth of his kindness. What could she fear, with Keith beside her?

His parents must have thought the same thing about each other, an insidious little voice whispered in her mind. At first love is blind and finds no fault. It's only later, when the bloom is off the rose, that regret sets in. . . .

"If they come, we'll hear them, but we'll be hidden from their sight," Keith said as they walked hand in hand to the waterfall, allowing its cooling spray to mist their bodies. He sat down first, and Stacy sank beside him.

He turned to her. "Remember the first night we sat in here? After I tipped the boat over?"

She smiled, though she knew he couldn't see her. "Yes."

"And the next night, and the waterfall we made love under? Remember that, my darling?"

She nodded. "Yes." The word was a sigh.

"That was the night I fell in love with you." He combed her hair with his fingers. "It scared the life out of me."

"I . . . know what you mean," she said uncertainly.

Rhythmically he stroked her head, kissing the crown. He smelled musky and desirable, and even though she couldn't see, she shut her eyes to concentrate on his scent.

"Stacy, I know you've been worried about . . . a lot of things. If it's any consolation, I have been too."

Her heart lurched. "Do you . . . want to call it off?" she asked in a strangled voice.

"Hey, no way," he murmured, trailing his fingers over her temple and cheek. "No way on earth."

Relief flooded through her. She pressed her head against his hand and turned her face to kiss it.

"You dear heart," he said feelingly. "Come on, honey. Let's start talking like two people who are about to be married."

"It makes me so happy to hear you say that. *Aloha au ia 'oe,* Keith."

In a rush of emotion they embraced. He cradled her head, rocking gently from side to side. As one body they inhaled, held their breath, exhaled.

A deep, abiding sense of peace welled up in Stacy. Olga was right. She had misplaced her priorities. This was what was important—sharing love, sharing yourself, joining your soul with another's in that magical, mystical chant called Life. This was the highest purpose she could serve. And this was why Keith, with his tremendous capacity to love, could never be considered a man who had wasted his life.

"It's going to be all right," she said.

"Yes. But we must talk. We've got to iron out as much as we can. Divorce isn't in my plans, Stacy. I saw what it did to my parents."

"Yes." And what it had done to him. She would never inflict that kind of pain on someone she loved, be it Keith himself or one of their children.

"First things first," he said, and they kissed long and deep. Stacy's face and scalp tingled. It seemed an eon since they had made love. Her hands traveled over him, searching out the buttons on his shirt, and he began to breathe harder as he fondled her breasts. Then he jerked away and held her hands, saying, "Later, my darling. We need to talk more than we need to make love." He laughed ironically. "I never dreamed *I'd* say something like that!"

"I never dreamed I'd be pawing at some guy." she said shyly.

" 'Some guy'? *'Some guy'*? I'm your fiancé, woman!"

They laughed. "Yes, you are. And yes, we should talk, so here goes." She considered. "How do we get started?"

"I suppose we should talk about the things that we're concerned about," he said simply.

She nodded, took a breath. "I'll go first. Um, where do you want to live after we get married?"

There was a pause. "Why, Stacy, I just assumed we—"

He was interrupted by a noise at the head of the cave.

Stacy raised her head. "What's that?" she whispered.

He laid his finger over her lips, then took her hand and tugged at it, so she would stand. Slowly they both rose and crept from behind the waterfall.

A voice wafted toward them. "This is insanity, Dr. Martin!" Stacy's eyes widened. It *was* Norman Du-Mont. And Dr. Martin had come with him. "We could be arrested."

"Shut up, Norman. Stacy Livingston wasn't born yesterday. As soon as they realize the notebook's missing, they'll be swarming all over this cave. This is our only chance."

"But, sir, the fish aren't even here yet."

"I know that, idiot! All we're doing is verifying her notes. And when she finds the fish, I'll take the credit. I'll say I sent her here myself."

"But, sir, what about me?"

"My funding's due to be reevaluated, Norman. If it comes through, there might be a position for you on my staff. After your thesis is approved, of course."

The two of them carried flashlights that lit up the interior of the cave, casting eerie shadows that flickered dangerously near the place where Keith and Stacy crouched. The two men sauntered toward the waterfall. Keith clasped Stacy's hand and urged her behind him. He positioned his body between her and the approaching intruders.

"And could I have my own office, sir?" Norman's voice was so loud that the hairs on the back of Stacy's neck prickled. It was all she could do to keep from crying out.

"Now, Norman, let's don't be greedy."

They walked past the waterfall. Keith spread a protective arm in front of Stacy.

"When do you think they'll discover the theft, sir?"

"Well, certainly not until tomorrow. She won't be using the notebook tonight, I would think. It's too late."

"Um. sir, I . . . had some trouble finding it," Norman said in an uneasy voice. "I had to . . . ah, look for it."

Dr. Martin stopped walking. "*What*? You mean you left evidence that you'd been there?"

"A little." Stacy couldn't help a gasp of indignation. A little!

Keith gave her hand a squeeze, pushed her gently backward and leaped toward the men.

"Stop!" he thundered. "Stop right there!"

"Dr. Martin, how could you?" Stacy demanded, bounding after Keith.

Dr. Martin and Norman froze, two pudgy, pale men with horn-rimmed glasses, and then Dr. Martin yelled, "Run!" and started scrambling up the boulders.

"Wait for me, Dr. Martin!" Norman yelled, but Stacy picked up a little rock and whacked him on the head. He buckled and fell.

"Uh-oh," Stacy murmured, staring down at him.

Meanwhile, Keith darted after Dr. Martin. The professor threaded his way among the stalactites and stalagmites. In his haste he stumbled and almost fell, then continued farther and farther up the wall to where the stalactites and stalagmites grew thicker. Fittingly, they hampered his way like the bars of a prison cell.

"Stand still, dammit!" Keith shouted. "I'm going to catch you anyway."

"Not without a fight!" Dr. Martin shot back. "Livingston, consider your thesis rejected!"

"Oh, balderdash!" Stacy cried, kneeling beside Norman and lightly slapping his face to rouse him.

"You're no scholar, Livingston!" Dr. Martin went on, frantically dodging Keith, who was closing in on him. "If you were, you'd share your—"

As he spoke, he flailed with his flashlight. It whacked against one of the stalagmites. There was a strange whirring sound, and then a click, and the stalagmite glided out of his reach.

"What's going on?" Norman asked, opening his eyes. "Wha' happened?"

"Lie still. You might have a concussion." Stacy picked up his flashlight and aimed it toward Keith and the professor.

The cave filled with thunder. The floor shook as if a volcano had erupted.

"Keith, Keith! What's happening?" Stacy cried, running toward him.

"Keep back!" he ordered over the cacophony. "I think the cave's exploding."

A shower of rocks rained in an arch above Keith and Dr. Martin. They shielded themselves, then ducked as the shower grew heavier.

There was a roar of noise that sounded like a groaning monster. Then, slowly, a portion of the cave began to disappear.

"Keith!" Stacy screamed. "Keith, are you all right?"

"Stacy, come up here!" Keith's voice was high, wildly urgent. "Quickly!"

She bounded up the rocks, grabbing onto a stalagmite to pull herself up.

She raced to Keith's side. "Look!" he shouted, pointing.

The back of the cave was actually a gigantic rock, and it was rolling away from them. Each minute turn made the earth tremble.

"There's something in there," Stacy said, straining to see into the darkness.

"Give me your flashlight," Keith said, taking it from her. He aimed it downward.

"Oh!" She clutched him in disbelief.

Below them in a small pit lay the rotting remains of a wooden crate. And among the splinters of ancient wood gleamed gold—piles of it, coins and bars, and tiaras and bracelets set with glittering gems.

"It's the treasure, *ipo*! We found the treasure!" Keith shouted, hugging Stacy. Maniacally, they danced in a circle, whooping and cheering, while Dr. Martin began to creep toward the shining fortune.

"Are those rubies and emeralds?" the professor asked excitedly.

"Watch it, Dr. Martin." Stacy waved a hand at him. "Or my fiancé will revoke *your* thesis!"

"Your fiancé?" Norman piped up behind them. "Stacy the Wondergrind has a fiancé? You've got to be kidding!"

Keith turned, but Stacy held him back. "Easy, Kika. He's in enough trouble already."

"Now we can wait for the Pele's Fire," Keith murmured. "The gods are watching out for us, my love."

Together they scrambled into the pit and examined the treasure. "This must be worth millions," Stacy crowed. "You're rich!"

Keith made a face. "The family isn't going to like this much. There'll be a lot left even after we pay my father's debts. We'll have to decide what to do with it." He dropped a pile of coins as if they were insignificant grains of sand. "And you and I have to decide what to do with each other."

She wrapped her arms around his waist. "I have a feeling we already know what to do with each other." They kissed.

"Livingston and a man," Norman said behind them. "I just don't believe it. I just don't believe it."

*   *   *

About an hour later, Kapono and Olga showed up. They had come to check on Stacy and Keith, and when they learned of the apprehension of the two thieves—and the discovery of the treasure—they boated to Tutu's and called the police.

As they were hauled away, Norman was contrite, Dr. Martin defiant.

"I'm really sorry, Livingston," Norman muttered. "I knew I wasn't a very good ichthyologist, and I was afraid Dr. Martin wouldn't pass me if I didn't help him."

"Spineless coward," Dr. Martin spat out. "If you'd broken into her apartment back home in the first place, none of this would have been necessary!"

The treasure was confiscated by the authorities for authentication and verification of ownership. Directed by Keith, the Mo'okini men took down the lights and the generator and helped Stacy bring in her own equipment for studying the fish.

Three nights before the time Stacy had calculated that the Pele's Fire were due to make their appearance, she and Keith settled down in the cave to resume their talk. It had become their special place, filled with memories and dreams and the sweet hours of getting to know each other.

"I had a revelation the night you got robbed," Keith said, unwrapping some mango pie and handing her a slice. "You said something to Olga: 'Thank you so much for not listening to me.' My Emerald Eyes, lately I've been trying to become what you said you—"

He stopped speaking and cocked his head. There was a whooshing sound, and the surface of the water grew so agitated, it looked as if it were boiling.

"Oh, great," Stacy groaned, running a hand through her hair. "What now?"

"What *now*? It's the Pele's Fire, Stace!" As she had instructed him, he grabbed a net and a portable holding tank and handed her a flashlight. "It's got to be!"

And it was. Dozens of them, perhaps hundreds,

sparkling and shining in the dim glow of Stacy's flashlight.

Lovely, lovely fish! Stacy clapped her hands in delight and picked up her camera. She snapped a dozen pictures in rapid succession.

"I did it! I did it!" she whispered fiercely, grinning at Keith. She kissed his cheek. "No, my love, *we* did it," she corrected herself. "Thank you Keith, so much."

The next day Keith called a press conference. Soon the news of Stacy's find was spanning the globe. Keith even contacted the governor of Hawaii, who flew in to congratulate Stacy. She was the ichthyologist of the hour.

Unfortunately, news of the treasure also leaked. To the dismay of the Mo'okinis, they were immediately besieged by requests for money. The family was overwhelmed, and Keith called an emergency *hui* meeting.

Keith and Stacy rowed to Tutu's to join the others, while policemen and family sentries guarded the school of fish.

"So," Tutu said as the meeting wore on. She was conducting the proceedings, as was her right as matriarch. "We have provided for Gerry's debts and set up trust funds for college for the kids. Maile wants a new washing machine and Pat's going to rewire his cabin. Nobody else wants anything and we still have almost a million dollars left. Now what? Who has an idea of what we should do?"

"I have a suggestion," Keith said, rising. "Let's give the money to Stacy for a research vessel. You know, like Jacques Cousteau. With her reputation, she should be able to attract all kinds of funds to further her research. She can become an international figure in ichthyology."

"Not some boring old professor in freezing Missouri," Kapono said.

"Michigan," Stacy corrected him dazedly.

Tutu beamed at Stacy. "What did I tell you about

my grandson, eh? Smart as they come. I think that's a perfect idea. What about everybody else? Any objections?"

"I don't want her to have it," Kapono said, frowning. He paused, then broke into a smile and added, "Unless she'll sign Olga and me on as her assistants."

"Oh, Kapono." Stacy took a breath, moved, and the two embraced.

"I figure as long as you're going to be a cousin of mine," he said, "I'd better get to know you. Nobody around here seems to remember, but I went to college too."

"For two semesters," Paulo pointed out.

"And got C's and D's," Pat Ching said.

Kapono shrugged. "Hey, who can study in a place like Hawaii? But I'll be a good worker, Stacy. I'll do whatever you want."

"Or Olga will beat you to a pup," Keith drawled, and everyone chuckled.

Stacy shook her head in disbelief. "I—I don't know what to say. I can't connect what you're saying with me. A research vessel?"

"Sure. We can even get Norman to work for you, I'll bet," Kapono said. "It's that or jail," he added in a theatrical aside. Again the family laughed.

Stacy glanced at Keith and saw that he looked troubled. She brushed stray tendrils of hair from her forehead and said quietly, "What about you, Keith?"

"I think it's time for us to have that talk," he replied, holding out his hand.

Tentatively she smiled. He didn't return it. A rush of fear dampened her euphoria. In the midst of all the happiness, something was wrong. Guardedly she took his hand. "All right."

"Go in peace, my dear ones." Tutu sighed. "What lovely great-grandchildren you will make for me."

Stacy blushed. Keith smiled sadly and rubbed her shoulder.

"We'll see, Tutu."

They walked out of the yard and into the dense stand of palms behind Menehune House.

The air was filled with the scent of flowers, as it had been the first day they'd met. And the sun was beginning to drop into the sea, a shimmering orange globe that tinged the bright blue sky with a soft shade of salmon.

"So, my dear one," Keith murmured, echoing Tutu's loving tone. "Now, at last, we have a moment alone." He put his arms around her. "I was going to say something about a week ago."

Stacy managed a smile. "I remember."

He took a deep breath before speaking. "I'm not a man made for shoes and suits and pens in my pocket protector. My dreams are simple. My wants are few."

Unsteadily she nodded. What was he trying to say? That they were ill-matched after all? That he'd changed his mind?

"I love Hawaii," he went on.

"Um," she said in a strangled voice. "Um, are you trying to say you don't want to leave?"

"No, I don't."

Like the cave, her world crashed on top of her. She hunched as though pelted by falling rocks and boulders. "I understand." Her voice was a croak.

He looked at her. "I'm not finish—"

"I achieved my ambition. I found the Pele's Fire, and the university is sure to award me my doctorate." Bravely, but with a sinking heart, she faced him. "If you want to live here, I can handle it, Keith. It's more important that we're together. If that's what you still want."

"Oh, honey. You're so far off the mark." Tenderly he wiped her eyes, bending down to make sure he didn't miss a single tear. Then he tousled her hair. "You silly *menehune*, you don't understand. I'm trying to tell you that sailing away with you on your research vessel will entail some sacrifice, but that you're worth it. I'm trying to tell you how much I love you."

"You . . . are?" She grabbed his wrists. "You . . . do?"

"If I can be your barefoot house husband, it'll be enough for me."

Her heart started beating again. She raised a hopeful face to him. "What?"

"I'll be your house husband. I'll do the cooking. I'll type your papers and check your references and make your phone calls and wait on you hand and foot."

"Wow!" She clutched at his shoulders as she stared at him in amazement. "Wow!"

He chuckled. "Yes, wow. It will be my pleasure to treat you like a princess. As long as you don't want to make a mainland businessman out of me. That's all I ask, Stacy. As well as the right to give you a massage once a week." He glanced at her firm stomach. "And maybe a baby or two, as the years pass?"

"Oh, Keith, of course! Three babies. Four!" She threw herself into his arms and bombarded his chin and neck with kisses. "Bend down!" she ordered, laughing, and pelted him with more kisses as he obeyed.

"Oh, you love me!" he cried, lifting her above him and gazing up at her. "You love me!"

"Yes! Yes, I do!" She tried to kiss him again. "And I always will."

He slid her down his front. He was happy, and his joy filled her with bliss. It was as if they were making love to each other's minds as they smiled, knowing they wanted each other mentally as well as physically. That they were one spirit, one soul, shining as if in a mirror, each for the other.

"Do you mind so much that I don't want to set the world on fire?" Keith whispered.

"No, my love. It's enough that you want to set *me* on fire."

"Good. No more trouble. Once more, peace and aloha reign on Golden Bay."

She laughed. "No more trouble."

They meandered back to Tutu's, stopping every few

yards to kiss. The sun had set by the time they returned, but everyone was still waiting for them.

Keith grinned at his grandmother. "Now, Tutu, about those great-grandchildren . . ."

Tutu clapped her hands in delight.

The men's voices chanted, and then the women's. The voices mingled, rose, grew. Their beautiful sound filled the Fern Grotto, traditional site of Kauai weddings. In the recessed amphitheater carved out of lava, a minister stood beside Keith, who was dressed in a white shirt and slacks, a red sash tied low on his hips, wearing a lei and a headband of white carnations and lavender crown flowers. Similarly attired, Kapono stood beside him, looking more nervous than the bridegroom. He and Olga would marry the following day.

Olga appeared, wearing a sunny yellow formal muumuu called a *holoku*. High-necked, with a short train trailing on the smooth stone, the gown revealed a femininity and beauty in Olga that Stacy had never seen.

With part of the treasure money, Tutu had flown Stacy's family in, and everyone was delighted with Keith and with Stacy's success. For the first time Stacy understood that her father had always loved her and been proud of her. He had simply had trouble telling her. And he and a merchant acquaintance of Keith's were discussing a business venture that could possibly pull him out of the financial difficulties he had faced all his life.

The chant continued, then changed into a vocal version of the traditional *Wedding March*. As Stacy began the sweet journey down the aisle, Tutu stood first, then Gerald and Nele, then Stacy's family and the rest of the *hui* Mo'okini and their friends.

As she and her father walked together, Stacy saw a tear slide down his lined cheek, and he gripped her hand tightly.

"Things are coming so right," he whispered. "You've done me proud, daughter."

"Thank you, Daddy," she murmured back. "You don't know what that means to me."

"You know, you're as pretty as your mother was on her wedding day."

She felt pretty, in her *holoku* of pure white silk, cut slightly off the shoulder and edged with lace. Her train was long and carried by a solemn Lani, who was excited about all the hoopla, but nervous about her responsibility to this vision in white, her new auntie. Stacy carried a huge bouquet of island flowers and wore a white carnation and lavender crown flower headband like Keith's in her free-flowing hair.

The song continued, swelling, proclaiming the love this man and woman bore for each other—a love that made the gods rejoice. A love so strong, it would see them through peril and disappointment, through the birth of their children and Stacy's career successes, and all the precious moments of their existence together.

Stacy stopped beside her mother and kissed her, then turned to Nele and Tutu, who carefully lifted leis of carnations, crown flowers, and jasmine over her head and also kissed her.

"Welcome, welcome," Tutu murmured, daubing at her eyes. "Aloha, my sweet Stacy."

The voices rose in a final chorus, filling Stacy's heart. Her father let go of her hand and she faced her bridegroom alone.

Keith's face glowed as his gaze locked with hers. Those eyes, she thought, that soon would look upon her in secret, as they made love as man and wife.

Those eyes that glittered unshed tears of love.

Those eyes that chanted, *Aloha, my sweet Stacy*. Aloha.

THE EDITOR'S CORNER

Santa's overflowing bag couldn't hold treats any sweeter or spicier than those in our LOVESWEPT bag of goodies next month!

First you have another delightful romance from Eugenia Riley whose **WHERE THE HEART IS,** LOVE-SWEPT #174, is set in sultry Natchez, Mississippi. Just imagine yourself in heroine Leigh Carter's shoes leading a tour of the glorious ante-bellum mansion in which she's boarding. You have in tow a group of lovely little old ladies, and you're regaling them with stories about the house. You open the door to a bedroom, continuing your spiel when you hear gasps and see several of the ladies swooning. Hmm-m. You LOVESWEPT readers are so shrewd that I'll bet you've guessed that the opened door revealed our hero, Peter Webster, a hunk, who is nearly naked (well, he *is* wearing a devilish grin!). From this unusual first meeting, Leigh and Peter proceed to discover the rare and wonderful qualities in each other. But Leigh has an enormous talent that she's kept secret and, like every secret and its reason for being, it profoundly threatens her intimate relationship with Peter. By turns humorous and serious, **WHERE THE HEART IS** features two characters we believe you will long remember!

Written with verve and dash, **EXPOSÉ,** LOVESWEPT #175, by Kimberli Wagner is a wonderfully off-beat romance, but one that has the traditional elements all of us love so well. In heroine Kate Polanski and hero Adam MacHugh, both hard working reporters, we meet two enormously spirited, passionate, downright believable people. These two have a long-running but cool feud going on in the newsroom when their editor dares to pair them to "get the story." And a dazzling, compli-

(continued)

cated story it is about stolen art and international jewel thieves. Every dangerous moment together Kate and Adam are falling wildly, madly in love with one another. Only a surprising truth . . . about the story and about themselves . . . brings them together, permanently, at last. **EXPOSÉ** is breathtakingly fast-paced and for me it evoked all the glamour and grit of one of those wonderful old Hepburn-Tracy films.

Iris Johansen is a wonder! Sometimes I have to pinch myself to be convinced I'm not dreaming that it was only in August and September of 1983 that we published Iris's first two books ever—and a "matched pair" at that. Who could have guessed that the publication of **STORMY VOWS** and **TEMPEST AT SEA** would start a trend? Iris virtually invented the continuing characters in series romance which is all the rage now. Here, next month, she continues to dazzle us with her marvelous imagination that produces whole new countries, languages, and tribes for us. Larger than life still, the members of her intertwined families and groups of friends breathe the breath of life for us. And so it is with **'TIL THE END OF TIME**, LOVESWEPT #176. We return to Tamrovia and to Sandor Karpathan, now the leader of a revolutionary army there, who discovers in Alessandra Ballard the woman who means more to him even than honor. The astonishing power of Sandor's and Alessandra's desire for one another is only tempered by the dangers they encounter from a wily and fierce opponent. As always, we know you will treasure this powerful romance from this powerful storyteller.

What better book to round out this celebratory season than the second novel by Linda Cajio? Her first, **ALL IS FAIR**, LOVESWEPT #145, was indeed a magnificent debut in romance writing, zooming straight to the Number One position on a national chain's bestseller list! And Linda will delight you again, we

(continued)

know, with **HARD HABIT TO BREAK,** LOVESWEPT #177. Heroine Liz O'Neal has a problem I am all too familiar with—cigarette smoking. She's determined to kick the habit and is smoking one of her three cigarettes of the day when gorgeous Matt Callahan catches her behind the shed! For a moment he thinks she's a teenager and starts to read the riot act to her . . . but one full look at the lady has him shut up and reeling! Matt is a living, breathing danger to Liz's peace of mind and her banker's image in their small town. The situation is all the worse because Matt is her next door neighbor. He is bold and brassy and a veritable devil . . . who soon has her in such a dither that she can scarcely add a column of figures or open a new account. This charmer of a love story is certain to make your holiday season very merry indeed.

We trust that our LOVESWEPTs next month won't interfere too much with shopping and gift wrapping!

For the fourth straight year we send you the same heartfelt message: May your New Year be filled with all the best things in life—the company of good friends and family, peace and prosperity, and, of course, love.

Warm wishes for 1987 from all of us at LOVESWEPT.

Sincerely,

Carolyn Nichols

Carolyn Nichols
   Editor
LOVESWEPT
Bantam Books, Inc.
666 Fifth Avenue
New York, NY 10103

A TIME FOR US

By E. V. Dolan
(25870-2 • $3.50)

Tragedy brought them together in the magnificent Vermont mountains, where a healing of their hearts began. But the two who met as strangers soon grew intimately close, attraction blossoming into the deepest kind of love. In one extraordinary year they filled every moment with a passion for life and each other. Their love, like the stars, was incandescent—and their only enemy was time.

Rich with all the ecstasies and sorrows of love, shimmering with the wild beauty of its natural setting, *A Time for Us* will linger in the mind and the heart long after the last page is turned.

For your ordering convenience, use the handy coupon below:

His love for her is madness.
Her love for him is sin.

Sunshine
and
Shadow

by Sharon and Tom Curtis

COULD THEIR EXPLOSIVE LOVE BRIDGE THE CHASM BETWEEN TWO IMPOSSIBLY DIFFERENT WORLDS?

He thought there were no surprises left in the world ... but the sudden appearance of young Amish widow Susan Peachey was astonishing—and just the shock cynical Alan Wilde needed. She was a woman from another time, innocent, yet wise in ways he scarcely understood.

Irresistibly, Susan and Alan were drawn together to explore their wildly exotic differences. And soon they would discover something far greater—a rich emotional bond that transcended both of their worlds and linked them heart-to-heart ... until their need for each other became so overwhelming that there was no turning back. But would Susan have to sacrifice all she cherished for the uncertain joy of their forbidden love?

"Look for full details on how to win an authentic Amish quilt displaying the traditional 'Sunshine and Shadow' pattern in copies of SUNSHINE AND SHADOW or on displays at participating stores. No purchase necessary. Void where prohibited by law. Sweepstakes ends December 15, 1986."

Look for SUNSHINE AND SHADOW in your bookstore or use this coupon for ordering: